THE RESURGENCE

RICK WOOD

BLOOD SPLATTER PRESS

ABOUT THE AUTHOR

Rick Wood is a British writer, born in Cheltenham.

His love for writing came at an early age, as did his battle with mental health. After defeating his demons, he grew up and became a stand-up comedian, then a drama and English teacher, before giving it all up to become a full-time author.

He now lives in Loughborough, where he divides his time between watching horror, reading horror, and writing horror.

I Do Not Belong

Death of the Honeymoon

Sean Mallon:

Book One – The Art of Murder

Book Two – Redemption of the Hopeless

The Edward King Series:

Book One – I Have the Sight

Book Two – Descendant of Hell

Book Three – An Exorcist Possessed

Book Four – Blood of Hope

Book Five – The World Ends Tonight

Non-Fiction

How to Write an Awesome Novel

Thrillers published as Ed Grace:

The Jay Sullivan Thriller Series

Assassin Down

Kill Them Quickly

1940

PRAGUE, THE CAPITAL OF CZECHOSLOVAKIA, WAS IN THE MIDST of death and chaos. Front doors were decorated with wreaths of murder, torture stuck to the light of the lampposts, and the desolate streets were consumed with suffering so extreme it could only have been imagined by the sickest of visionaries.

Istvan couldn't help but feel responsible.

Which was, of course, because he *was* responsible.

He closed his eyes, twisted his head away, as if shutting out the world would somehow shut out the truth.

But he couldn't shut it out; nor could he disguise it or hide from it. The burden of knowledge was always there, always tormenting him, and no matter how much he tried to turn away from the sea of his thoughts, he could still hear the souls drowning in the ocean of his guilt.

He forced himself to open his eyes and look out the window. He forced himself because he had to see what his selfish actions had caused, as if the pain of seeing the suffering would be a sufficient enough punishment to stop the cruelty of his remorse.

It wasn't. The sights remained, as did the blame.

To watch a group of uniformed strangers torture families in the most inhumane of ways...

To watch this, and to know it was because of him, because of the evil he had allowed to enter this world...

To watch with a painful awareness what a little nudge from Hell had done, knowing that it was because of him meddling with things he had not understood at the time...

He understood it all too well now.

It wasn't that those swastika-bearing bastards weren't in control of what they were doing. He would not remove humanity's contribution from the equation, just as he would not remove responsibility from the man who pulled the trigger – but Istvan knew: *for humans to commit inhumane acts, a push is required by great evil.*

Three soldiers lined up a family of six beside the river. Istvan watched from his warm protection, high up in the building, hidden from those who had sought him out, as the soldiers demanded that the family remove their shoes.

The family clung onto each other, shivering from fear and frost. The first soldier fired a bullet through their aligned heads, not wanting to waste what they needn't waste.

The two parents fell into the river.

The four children were too small to meet the same bullet, so they met another two; one from either side. Their empty vessels followed their parents into the water.

The soldiers collected the shoes and placed them in a bag, then walked on like nothing had happened. Like it was a normal day at work. Like they were about to go on a coffee break.

Istvan wanted to retch, but he didn't deserve to.

Instead, he turned away, withdrawing his hands from the curtains and allowing the small shaft of light to disappear, returning the room to complete darkness. The furniture he'd spent a lifetime acquiring still lay scattered in discarded, unrecognisable pieces of splintered wood.

He hadn't repaired anything.

There was no point.

He hobbled through his home and into the kitchen, where he lit the stove. He filled a rusty kettle with water and placed it upon the flames. The stove cast a small, amber light. He would normally avoid lighting it in order to avoid attracting attention from outside, but today, he did not care.

There was little that would make him care anymore.

So imagine they found him. Then what?

If they hung him or shot him or beat him to death – what difference would it make?

It wasn't any less than he deserved, after all.

He made his cup of tea with his final tea bag and took his steaming mug through to the living room, where his armchair still remained intact amongst the battered features of the room.

He sat in it, as he once had so peacefully.

He closed his eyes.

Enjoyed his chair one last time.

Thought about those who had come and gone in his life. Such as his wife, whom he had loved very much – possibly too much. He had risked everything to save her from her illness. Medicine and hospitals hadn't worked. Neither had more extreme medicine, nor the first spirits he called upon, nor first touch of evil that tempted his desperation.

He had been willing to sell his soul to the demonic – but they just laughed and took it anyway.

And, with his absence from Earth to beg great evil for great mercy, great evil had been allowed to spread.

It started with politics. Then hospitals, workhouses, orphanages. The rise of the demonic had been more than he could fight. A single demon in a body with the assistance of a priest had been doable – to take on a world spreading with lost souls was impossible.

And now, here they were.

A year later, and the invasions started.

Genocide spread throughout the world.

The great evil had already killed millions, and millions more were to come.

All for his selfish love.

All in the quest to rid the one he loved of an illness that only intensified her pain the more intensely he tried.

And now here he was.

Watching the world erupt.

Watching evil spread. All that bad men had needed to become evil men was a little extra evil in the world to encourage them on their way.

He couldn't bear to think about it anymore.

If one single person could change the course of time so much, then that person should be removed from the pages of history. That person does not have a place on Earth, and he must leave Earth in hope that Earth could find some semblance of peace in his absence.

He finished his tea.

Placed the mug on the floor. For the first time in his life, he wasn't going to entertain his compulsive need for cleanliness. He was going to let it sit on the coarse tufts of the carpet and drip its remnants until a small pool gathered and made absolutely no difference to the wreckage of his home.

In his final act, he lifted his thick journal and filled in its final pages. He signed it and placed it away in a chest he knew only the right people would look in.

He trudged up the stairs, his steps heavier than they had been in weeks. He didn't mind the creaks now. Before, creaks could mean he could get discovered. Now, creaks just announced his walk to the gallows.

He found it in his bedroom. The rope hung to the light. A noose prepared days ago for this moment.

He would have done it then if he'd had the guts.

But he hadn't. He had thought he could fix it, that he could stay in this world and right his wrongs, rectify the great mistake.

But he couldn't watch so many die and so many suffer for his actions.

It had taken less than a year for the world to be lost to Hell.

How long would it take for Hell to be found on Earth?

He stepped onto the stool. Placed his head neatly in the hole. Squeezed the rope tighter. Pulled it until he couldn't breathe.

Closed his eyes.

Kicked out the stool.

He immediately wished he had chosen a quicker option. But he had no gun and he had no pills; he had no way of doing this besides suffocating himself.

His throat tightened and his breath escaped. His body desperately wheezed for oxygen; the autonomic response of his body rather than his own intention.

Soon, it went black.

He fell into unconsciousness before his neck broke.

His neck broke only seconds before he died.

He left the world he had destroyed to tear itself apart in his absence for a great many years to come.

NOW

2

A FEW PEOPLE DRESSED IN BLACK WERE SCATTERED ACROSS THE first few pews. Oscar glanced over his shoulder, hoping he'd find more people in attendance, but he didn't. He was sad for the turnout, but not surprised. He had never known Julian to speak about family or to socialise with other friends. In fact, he wondered who these few people were, considering they were faces he hadn't seen in the good few years he'd known Julian.

"Julian Barth," the priest spoke, "was a leader to his friends and a surrogate brother to April, the younger sister he'd always wanted and finally found."

Oscar glanced at April beside him, who had kept her eyes focussed directly ahead for the entire service. She hadn't looked at him, or anyone else – he wasn't sure she'd even looked at the priest. She'd just held her empty gaze, her eyes wide open, her face poised with little emotion.

Some people may have found her lack of expression cold. He knew better. This was her trying to hold it together, knowing that if she met someone else's eyes she would probably cry.

Oscar wanted her to cry.

She hadn't yet, and he knew she needed to.

She had looked close to it on the night she found Julian's body, when he was awoken by her scream. He'd looked from the corpse to her, awaiting her reaction, those tears accumulating in the corners of her eyes – but that's where they had stayed. Shock took over, and she barely moved until the police and ambulance left hours later.

He reached his hand over and placed it in hers. She didn't move her hand to accommodate his, but she didn't flinch away, either. He gave her a gentle squeeze. She didn't acknowledge it. She stayed still. He retracted his hand and returned it to his own lap.

He wished he knew what she wanted.

Did she want his reassurance? His affection? Did she desire his hand in hers, whether or not she asked for it or welcomed it?

Or did she want to be left alone? Did she want her solace, her peace, her time to grieve without interference?

Oscar hoped that, should she want to be alone, she would want to be alone with him. Time away from other people had always meant 'all people but Oscar.'

But he wasn't sure that was the case anymore.

It hurt, though he didn't let on. Because he knew this wasn't about him. This was about her. This was about her pain, and how she wanted to deal with it, and he couldn't be selfish, he couldn't allow his own ego or need for her reassurance to affect the way he tried to be there for her.

But he also needed her back.

Not just for him, but for the fight. She was an integral part of what they were trying to do, and he needed her to return to full strength quicker than one would expect under such dire, violent, tragic circumstances.

There were always casualties in war. Julian had said so himself. He wouldn't have wanted this.

Then again, Oscar imagined Julian wouldn't have wanted death, either.

Sometimes, we just can't get what we want.

And sometimes, what we want comes at a cost.

The state of the world was as a result of Oscar's actions, after all. In his desperation to save April from an attacking demon, he had entered a realm that was not of this world in order to save her. This had meant that there were no longer any prominent Sensitives present on Earth to balance the equation between Heaven and Hell, and Hell had taken the opportunity to enter Earth and upset the balance and increase demonic presence to a catastrophic level. Ever since then, mass demonic possession had ensued, diabolical acts of murder and torture were increasing rapidly, and there was not a country or person unaffected. After all, when people are given a push by Hell, they commit acts that they would only be tempted to do in their darkest moments.

They were running out of time to do anything, and this was why he needed April to recover quickly and re-join the fight as soon as possible. After around a year of a person being possessed, amalgamation incarnation occurs – meaning the demon entwines with the person inside the body they are occupying, removing the soul in its entirety, and taking that person's place on Earth. After that, there would be nothing an exorcism could do – and if they didn't do something to eradicate the mass possession that was so rapidly growing, then all these demons would amalgamate, and genocide and torture, and every act of conceivable evil, would occur in ways that the world had not yet seen.

It would mean the twisted, violent end to the human race.

But there was hope, and that hope was found in a girl called

Thea. Just seventeen, but a Sensitive whose gift was extraordinarily strong.

Oscar feared, however, that this gift was still not strong enough. She could rid a building of its demons, but saving a building was still far off from saving the world.

"We now ask if April would be kind enough to step forward and say a few words she has prepared," the priest spoke, and stepped back.

April remained seated.

Her eyes remained forward, her body remained still, her heart kept on thudding; the only sound louder than her slow, wheezing breath.

"April," Oscar whispered.

She didn't move.

Then she did – but only to bow her head, to close her eyes, to resist all impulse to show how she really felt.

Oscar reached into her jacket pocket and withdrew the words she had solemnly prepared.

"Perhaps you could read them," Oscar requested, handing the piece of paper to the priest.

The priest looked sympathetically to April, then to Oscar, and took the notes.

"I would be honoured," the priest said, unravelling the paper and resuming his place at the pulpit.

"These are the words, as written by April," the priest said, then placed some glasses upon the end of his nose and began reading. "I first met Julian as a wayward teenager, with nowhere to go and no one to care for me."

Oscar tuned the priest out, putting his arm gently on April's back.

"Are you okay?" he whispered.

It was a stupid question, he knew.

Of course she wasn't.

He just needed her to talk. To say something. To show that she was present in this moment in any way she was willing.

"April?" he tried again, as quietly as he could.

Her lips tightened and he saw them quiver. He placed a tissue in her hand. She scrunched it in her fist and held it next to her face, ready for the moment that the tears came.

But they didn't.

Oscar wished they would, but they didn't.

"It's okay," he told her. "It's okay to be upset. If you–"

She raised her hand and gently waved it.

He stopped talking and took his arm back, leaving April to her despair.

He wished he knew what she needed him to do. He wished she'd tell him. Let him know somehow.

He wished a lot of things.

The priest concluded the speech.

"April and Oscar would also like me to remind you that there will be some light food put on in the Coat of Arms, which is found if you turn left from the church, and up the road."

The priest brought the service to an end. The casket was closed, and four strangers carried it out to the car, ready to be taken to the crematorium.

April walked down the aisle before Oscar had even stood. He tried to go after her, but halted, not knowing if that was the right thing to do, and watched her disappear out the church.

He had said he'd go to the crematorium with her, but by the time he stepped outside, the car had already left.

3

THEA FELT HER MOTHER'S EYES BURNING INTO THE BACK OF HER head, but she did her best to ignore it. She shoved a pile of clothes into her suitcase, a few tattered books she knew by heart, and a teddy that she gave a gentle kiss to before placing on the top.

"But I don't understand," her mother kept insisting. "It all sounds a bit…"

Thea turned and raised her eyebrows.

"Delusional?" she offered, as an end to the sentence. "Ridiculous? Crazy? Stupid, mental, or pathetic, even?"

"No, just… farfetched."

Thea snorted a laugh. Only her mother could describe Thea's need to play a key role in stopping the end of the world as far-bloody-fetched!

Thea pulled the zip around the suitcase, pressing down upon it with her knee to allow the zip to find its way around.

"Why don't you just stay here?" her mother suggested, her voice sounding that way a mother's voice does when they know they are not going to break through their child's stubbornness. It was a weak enough proposal as it was, only weakened more by the adding of, "You can do all your fun and games here, can't you?"

"Fun and games?" Thea repeated, hands on hips, and saw her mother instantly realise she had said the wrong thing.

"Oh, I didn't mean it like that."

"How did you mean it?"

"Oh, I, just – maybe it would be better if you saw a doctor. You've had a lot of stress. I know it's not been easy, and me and your father have struggled to understand, honestly we have – but you running away is not–"

"This is not me running away. Before, it was me running away – but I'm telling you what's happening now. This is me leaving."

"Then don't leave. Please."

Thea dragged the suitcase past her mother and through the hall. She stopped at the smallest bedroom and looked inside. Everything was still as it was, every toy scattered on the floor, every piece of the dinosaur wallpaper, every boyish book on wrestling. It was all here.

Her mother appeared over her shoulder.

"See, we lost your little brother; don't let us lose you too."

Thea's muscles tightened. She could feel the strain of her self-restraint fighting the urge to say a hundred hurtful things.

How dare she use him against her. It was not fair.

"This doesn't have to mean you losing me," Thea said. "And if I'd known all this a few months ago, he'd still be here."

She marched through the hallway, down the stairs, and to where her shoes lay beside the door, trailed incessantly by her mother. As she did her shoelaces, she could feel her mother hovering, looking for the right thing to say.

"Stop it," Thea said, finishing the last loop and standing. "I can see you trying to think of how to stop me from leaving, but it's not going to work. I'll be safe. I'll be fine. You just... need to let me go."

"But... you're only seventeen. You're my little girl."

Thea stepped forward. For the first time in the exchange, she smiled. She hugged her mum, but only for a few seconds.

"I'm not, though," she said. "I'm not your little girl. Not anymore."

"You're right. You are, you're right. You're a woman now. But I still love you. And I still think you should stay."

Thea smiled again.

"I love you, Mum," she said, and turned to the door handle.

"Thea, please."

Thea left, glancing at her watch. If she caught the next bus, she could be back for the wake. She wanted to show her support to April; after all, she wouldn't be the person she felt herself becoming if it weren't for her.

She turned back and saw her mum in the doorway. She waved.

Her mum gave a hesitant wave back.

Then she turned the corner and her childhood home disappeared from view.

4

Normally, when in a social situation that involved a buffet, Oscar would be self-conscious about overloading his plate, not wanting to stop others from enjoying the sausage rolls and cheese-with-pineapple-sticks and assortments of crackers.

But, honestly, it didn't seem as if there were that many takers. The pub had cordoned off part of its premises for them, and that space was filled with sparsely placed people, loitering without intent, staring aimlessly at anywhere but each other. There were a few that indulged in small talk, but most showed their respects by being present whilst aimlessly vacant in an uncomfortable silence.

Oscar watched April from afar. Sat in the corner. An untouched glass of vodka and Coke sat neatly on a coaster. She stared at the glass but didn't see it. So still, she could be dead.

For the first time in their relationship, he had no idea what to say to make things better; if there was even anything to be said. Every move he made toward her seemed redundant, every arm around her shunned, and every comforting whisper discarded like the life she was mourning.

The best thing to do was give her time, he knew that – but he wished he could guess what he should do in that moment.

He tried to imagine how he'd be feeling. Of course, he was in pain from the loss of a friend – albeit a resentful, angry one – but he couldn't imagine losing someone with the history and connection April had with Julian.

The door opened and Thea entered, wiping sweat from her brow. The sun was glaring through the windows, though Oscar could feel none of the heat in the well-air-conditioned pub.

"Hey," she said, smiling weakly. "How'd it go?"

It was an odd question to answer about a funeral.

"It was a nice service. A fitting tribute. And there's plenty of food left."

Thea looked around, finding April sitting in the corner.

"She okay?"

Oscar went to give an answer, but found that he didn't have one, so he just shrugged.

"I'm not entirely sure. Can I get you a drink?"

Wanting to divert the attention from how useless he felt, he went to the bar and ordered her a pint of amber ale – a surprise choice, as far as Oscar was concerned; he hadn't thought of her as an ale person.

"I'm going to go say hey," Thea said, taking her drink and walking toward April.

Oscar nodded and watched as Thea sat beside the woman he loved. He couldn't tell what they were saying, but he could imagine the conversation as Thea asked how April was doing; April didn't respond. Thea put her arm around April, and April's face scrunched into a contorted resistance to her tears. April took the first sip of her drink; an obvious avoidance tactic.

Thea gave April a hug.

Then Thea said something else. Something like, *do you want me to stay,* or, *would you like some space?*

A feeble nod from April prompted a reluctant rub of her back from Thea, and Thea returned to Oscar's side.

"She seems…" Thea said, then drifted off as Oscar's expression confirmed he knew what she meant.

"It's to be expected, I guess," Oscar said. "She needs time."

He wished he could come up with something more profound than the tired clichés that kept coming out of his mouth. *Life is short,* and, *death takes no prisoners,* and, *everything happens for a reason* – all statements that sound like they mean something, but do nothing but fill the silence.

"They were close, huh?"

Oscar nodded grudgingly.

"How's she been the past week? It could just be that it's the day of the funeral."

"She's been…" How could Oscar answer that? How had she been? "She's… she's been April. Strong and stubborn. Fearless and forthright. And never one to admit her suffering."

"Has she not spoken about it?"

Oscar hesitated. "Only in a passing way. Like, organising arrangements for today, monotone conversations with the paramedics… no talk of how she's actually feeling."

"Has she even cried yet?"

"Not…when she thinks she's being watched. But, when she's alone… The other day I did my teeth and I paused outside the bathroom and I could hear–"

Oscar had to stop for fear of tears himself. He bowed his head, and Thea momentarily put her arm around him.

"So what now?" Thea asked.

"Well, once everyone's gone, we'll pack up the buffet and–"

"No, I mean, in terms of the war. What now?"

Oscar looked at her peculiarly.

"I don't understand the question," he answered. "We carry on. We keep fighting. Same as we have been doing."

"And the new recruits? We have about fifty of them. The Church has arranged their accommodation, and we have a few more arriving today."

"We teach them. And we teach them fast."

"Do you really think we stand a chance?"

Oscar avoided giving a quick answer. Instead, he mulled over the question.

Do you really think we stand a chance?

In the end, he decided it was not a question he wished to answer, and Thea seemed to accept that, leaving them to sip on their drinks in thoughtful contemplation.

5

The instant Henry placed his foot off the coach and onto the wet pavement of the station, he was overwhelmed with anxiety once again. Taking his first bus ride, alone, at fourteen years old, had been scary enough – now he had to find a way from the bus to the accommodation.

He wished his parents were there, then remembered how much he didn't. They had been so proud of him when they'd discovered that he was a... what was it... a Sensitive?

They were devout Catholics and had forced him to spend most weekends of his childhood listening to them preach in the middle of a busy town centre about the righteous, and about how the end was nigh. He would sit and watch at a nearby bench, often agreeing with the occasional person who was bold enough to tell them to shut up. So they had inevitably been elated when word from the Church came – not just because Henry was going to fight in the war against the upcoming apocalypse, but this finally confirmed all that they'd been preaching for years.

Honestly, they couldn't have been prouder.

Henry wished they could have been as proud when he was

awarded his swimming badges, or when he got an A on his science test, or when he did his first cello recital. But their smiles had been mild compared to the beams that shone down upon him after they received this news.

In all honesty, Henry had never really bought into his parents' teachings. It had all seemed quite farfetched, quite extreme. He kept on asking questions they couldn't answer and was always met with the same response: a smile, and a reminder of the definition of the word *faith*.

Would he dare tell them about his doubts?

Would he heck!

If they didn't disown him there and then, he imagined he would remain in their lives as a constant burden. They would harness their resentment toward him until the day they died.

So, in that sense, he was grateful to be away.

But, stepping out of the coach station and into the busy streets of Gloucester town centre, he wished they could be with him just for a moment, just long enough to tell him what to do next. There were masses of people wearing big rugby shirts, all swarming to his right. There must be a match on or something.

He pressed himself up against a wall to avoid being in anybody's way. They were taking up the whole pavement and he didn't want to provoke anyone; despite most of them looking friendly, or with kids, or laughing and joking the way one does with a friend on a pleasant Saturday afternoon.

He could ask someone for directions.

As soon as the thought entered his mind, he shooed it away. He wasn't going to ask anyone anything. He wasn't even going to make eye contact.

There was a taxi rank behind him, at the edge of the bus station.

He began to edge forward, then stopped, not knowing what to say to the driver.

He really didn't want to have to speak to them.

He felt in his pocket for the wallet full of money his mum had given him. It had numerous, crisp twenty-pound notes in, waiting to be spent.

But how much was a taxi?

Yes, he easily had a few hundred in there – but what if that wasn't enough?

He shook his head. He'd ask beforehand how much it would be.

But then that would involve more conversation.

No, he'd risk it. Surely it wouldn't be more than a few hundred. Would it?

He took a deep breath, told the taxi driver where he wished to go, then sat in the back. The whole drive he kept feeling for his wallet, feeling for the notes, dreading the cost. What would the driver do if he didn't have enough?

Finally, the driver pulled up and turned over his shoulder.

"Six fifty," he said.

Feeling relief pass through him, he handed over a twenty and collected his change, then shuffled quickly out of the car.

There, before him, was a building with rows and rows of windows. Was this where he was going? What did he do now? How did he even get in?

He walked along the edge of the building, searching for the door, walking quickly around one corner, to the next, to the next – until he found himself approaching the same point where he had arrived. Just before he reached his original starting position, he found the entrance – mere steps from where he had originally arrived.

He entered to find a small lobby and an angry-looking woman sat behind a computer. He approached her cautiously, staring at her, waiting for the moment to talk but having no idea what to say.

"Hi?" she said.

"Hi," he responded, feeling the shake in his voice. "I'm... staying here... I think..."

"Name?"

"Henry Spelling."

She clicked her mouse a few times, typed something into the keyboard, then took an envelope from the drawer.

"Floor three, room twenty. Stairs are over there." She didn't point or indicate in any direction.

Henry took the envelope and looked around. Eventually, he found the stairs over the woman's shoulder and went up them warily, until he found floor three.

As soon as he entered the floor, he was taken aback by the smell of damp and burnt bacon. To his left was a kitchen, where shouts and loud conversation and big laughter came from. Luckily, he needed to go to his right.

He found his room, entered it, and locked the door behind him.

It was like a box, almost exactly the same size as his room from home. There was no toilet, so he'd have to use the shared one. There was a desk and a single bed. He dropped his bag to the floor, peered out the window, then lay on the bumpy mattress.

He stayed very still, staring at the ceiling, willing his thoughts to quiet down.

6

OSCAR STOPPED THE CAR, BUT NEITHER OF THEM STEPPED OUT.

He killed the engine and waited for the sound of its whirring to cease. Once it did, he made no effort to remove the key.

He turned to April, slowly and deliberately. Her elbow was against the frame of the open window, and her head rested on her hand.

Oscar reached his hand across and placed it on her leg.

"You're doing really well," he told her, though he wasn't sure if it was true. "It's been a tough day."

April nodded.

Oscar wondered whether to say more. Against his better judgement, his voice seeped out of him with little conviction and quiet enough that he could pretend he never said anything: "I wish you'd talk to me, though."

She looked down.

"Or just look at me."

He reached his hand across and placed it on the side of her face. She placed both her hands around his and held tightly;

such a simple gesture, but so needed. Suddenly, Oscar felt a little less useless.

She went to speak, but she didn't.

He didn't fill the silence. He waited, knowing she would speak eventually.

"I just..." she attempted. "I just can't believe he's gone."

Oscar resisted the temptation to give advice. Instead, he just listened and acknowledged.

"He's been such a constant for so long. I knew there would be casualties, it just..."

"...it doesn't seem real?"

She finally turned to look at him. Her eyes were glazed, but no tears fell. It felt good to be able to finish her sentence again.

"If you don't want to do the lecture later, we can tell the recruits–"

"No." She raised her hand in objection. "It can't wait."

"I could do it if you'd–"

"Honestly, Oscar, I just need to..."

She didn't finish her sentence. He didn't need her to.

"Come on," he said, and stepped out of the car. Together they made the short walk down the path to Julian's flat.

April fumbled the keys, dropping them as she searched for the right one. Oscar took them, smiling at her, found the right key, and they entered.

The flat was a mess. Julian had been living with them for a while, so they knew this was just a place of storage, but they didn't expect it to be so full of junk. Piles of boxes stacked against the wall, plastic bags of papers scattered around the floor, and a few dirty plates left in the sink.

April snorted a laugh, but only briefly.

"Typical Julian," Oscar offered. "Leaves us his washing up to do."

She forced a smile and he gave her a one-arm hug.

He watched as she meandered through to one bedroom, then to the other.

She emerged seconds later, stepping over various bits of clutter.

"I don't even know where to start with this."

Oscar stepped forward and took both of her hands in his.

"Why don't you concentrate on the training? I'll sort this."

"Really? It's a lot."

"It's fine." He handed her the car keys. "You go."

She gave him a soft, lingering kiss – the kind that still made him tingle – but the look she gave him afterwards did not reflect his relief. They had a brief moment of eye contact, then she looked away, as if she should feel guilty. As if she shouldn't be happy. As if it wasn't right that they shared affection when she should be in such pain.

Without touching him, she left.

He tried not to think about it. Tried to focus on the task at hand, looking around at the mass of junk and wondering where the hell to start.

7

A MASS OF FACES, MOST OF THEM YOUNG, SOME OF THEM NOT, all stared back at April with an expectation she felt she could never live up to.

Some of them knew what they were doing there. Some of them had been told to come and learnt as they were going along. Some were sceptics, some were not, and some appeared permanently bemused – but one thing they all had in common was that each and every one of them stared at April, awaiting her guidance.

"For those of you who are new," she said, trying to steady the shake in her voice, "welcome. For those who aren't…"

She forgot what she was about to say.

"Well… welcome back. My name is April, and I am what we refer to as a conduit."

She tapped the space bar of her laptop. The PowerPoint projecting onto the screen changed to a slide displaying a definition of the word *conduit*.

"Conduit," April read, then gulped, "is a channel for conveying water or other fluid."

She turned back to the faces. All of them so intent, so eager, so keen to be imparted knowledge upon. None of them had any idea about the severity of the war they were about to be plunged into. She both envied them and felt sorry for them.

Some of them may not even make it.

Some of them…

She realised she'd left too long a gap of silence.

"When it comes to mediumship, you must remember that you are the channel. The spirit is the water, or the fluid. And they are conveyed through you. They speak through you, and you are temporarily absent in your body."

"So you leave your body?" one curious voice shouted out.

The question took April by surprise, and she tried not to appear flustered.

"No, you do not. Imagine your body is a car. You simply move to the backseat and let something else drive for a while. You are still in that car – but you cannot control it, nor can you see out of the windscreen as well as the person in the front."

"Isn't that kinda risky?"

April hesitated. This wasn't supposed to be a question-and-answer session. This was supposed to be her teaching.

"What is your name?" April inquired.

"Rebecca," the girl answered.

"Right, Rebecca." April took a moment to compose herself. "If you have a question, I suggest you put your hand up. I have a lot to get through, and I may well end up covering what you wish to ask."

Rebecca put her hand up.

"Yes?" April prompted with a sigh.

"I just wanted to know – isn't it kinda risky? Like, giving control of your body to something evil."

"*Potentially* evil," April replied. "Not everything you channel will be evil – sometimes it will be a spirit, or a dead person, someone who has failed to move on. You should rarely ever channel a demon unless you have very good reason to, and you have experienced Sensitives around you ready to bring you back when needed."

April looked at the girl, who looked back blankly.

"Does that answer your question? Can I go back to the lesson now?"

Rebecca nodded.

April turned back to the slide and, out of the corner of her eye, she noticed Rebecca grinning at the boy next to her.

"Not all Sensitives are conduits, of course. Some of you are exorcists. Some of you are able to feel something in the room. Once you realise what your gift is, you can start to explore it. For example..."

April clicked to the next slide, and a picture of Oscar appeared, mid-exorcism.

"Oscar is part of our team, and he is a very gifted exorcist."

She clicked to the next slide. Thea appeared – a picture of her smiling at the camera.

"Thea is a newer, but integral part of what we are doing. She has displayed abilities of a Sensitive that, despite our many gifts, none of us will match."

She clicked to the next slide.

Julian appeared.

"And this is–"

She halted.

Stared.

She'd created this PowerPoint presentation before...

And she hadn't expected to...

She had to hold it together. Had to ensure the recruits did not see her break.

"This is... Julian," she spoke feebly, then decided to just move on to the next slide.

Rebecca's hand went up.

April tried to ignore it.

"A few examples of entities I have channelled," she began.

Rebecca's hand went even higher and even stiffer.

"Yes?" April said, not bothering to hide the exasperation from her voice.

"I was just wondering – has a Sensitive ever died from using their gift?"

April stared back at Rebecca, glaring intently.

It was as if the girl knew.

HENRY, LIKE ALMOST EVERY OTHER ONE OF THE FIFTY OR SO recruits sat in the lecture theatre, felt a wave of tension spread through them. People shifted, glanced at each other, but no one dared speak.

He stared at Rebecca.

He stared at April.

He watched as April did her best to compose herself, biting her lip, leaning her hands on the table and taking a deep breath. She closed her eyes, but just for a moment, then locked eyes with Rebecca.

"Yes," April finally answered, deep and gravely, full of resentment.

"And what hap–"

"I think I am done taking questions for now," April interrupted. "If you could be quiet now, that would be brilliant."

Rebecca looked momentarily taken aback and she backed down. She looked around, confused.

April seemed to notice this reaction. She straightened up, looked away from the many prying eyes, and turned back. She cast her eyes over everyone, passing through every face staring back at her.

"I'm going to be honest with you," April decided.

Henry wished that she wouldn't be.

For he felt he knew what was coming.

"Not everyone who's fought this war has survived. We have lost people." She took another deep breath. "*Good* people."

She went back a slide, and the picture of the man she didn't say much about reappeared.

"This is Julian," she said, a quiver wrecking the conviction her voice had achieved. "He died two weeks ago. He took his own life, but not of his own free will – a demon managed to somehow control his actions. We aren't sure how a demon got in, considering the preventative measures we took, but..."

April had to stop. She covered her face, then turned back to everyone with a renewed assertion.

"But Julian knew what was most important. He knew that this war was more than our lives. And if you don't realise that, then the door's over there. Please use it."

She looked around, waiting for someone to get up.

Henry wanted to.

Boy, Henry wanted to.

But he couldn't.

His own self-consciousness prevented him from walking out with everyone staring him, even if it meant escaping possible death, and he hated himself for how his desperate need not to be noticed always seemed to set his path to self-destruction.

"And he's not the only one we've lost," April continued.

April locked eyes with Rebecca, and Henry looked between them, frantically awaiting whoever would back down.

"Does that answer your question?" April asked, though there was only ever going to be one answer.

"Yes."

"Good. Now shut up, keep your hand down, and listen."

Rebecca nodded.

April returned to the slides and kept talking, but Henry heard little of it.

He had never realised his parents had sent him to a potential death.

This was far from what he wanted.

Suddenly, he felt so very far away from home.

As he stood amongst the endless mess, Oscar had to keeping reminding himself he was doing this to help April.

It was better for him to do it, he supposed. Not that Oscar didn't have a friendship with Julian – but they hadn't always seen eye to eye, and it was unlikely there'd be an item that would prompt fond memories lost forever. But for April, there could be a mug given as a gift, a photo at the bottom of a box, or even a discarded banana peel that reminded them of a joke from long ago that only they shared – ready to prompt further recollections and further despair.

In a way, Oscar was tempted to show April those things, hoping they would force her to show her grief and confront the feelings she kept hiding. But maybe that wouldn't be such a great idea and would end up being cruel rather than helpful.

The first few boxes were old books and VHS tapes. He tried to remember when the last time he'd seen a VHS tape was, and wondered how many more boxes were full of useless items Julian had pointlessly hoarded. Some of the books were ridiculously old; he recognised the book titles, but the covers were tattered and outdated.

He decided to make a 'to throw' pile, a 'to keep' pile, and a 'charity shop' pile.

Within an hour, his 'to keep' pile was almost empty, the 'charity shop' pile was a small mess, and the 'to throw' pile was a large mass of clutter.

Feeling parched, he searched through the cupboards for tea bags.

They had just been restocked.

Oscar abruptly felt quite upset.

Inside the fridge, a full, unopened carton of milk awaited him, along with half a takeaway curry saved for the next day's lunch. This wasn't the fridge of someone planning to take their own life. Julian would not waste time restocking his fridge if he wasn't planning on using its contents. Even in suicide, he'd avoid pointless inconveniences.

This only made what they had assumed all the truer – Julian's suicide had not been his own decision.

He had been coerced. By demonic influence.

He must have been.

Which led to the question...

How?

Julian was the least vulnerable out of all of them. April was a conduit and opened herself up to the risk of demonic influence on a daily basis. Thea was far too powerful to be so easily susceptible. And Oscar never took anywhere near as many precautions as Julian had.

So how had something gotten into him?

And how had they not noticed?

Demons don't just grab hold of someone and instantly destroy them. They creep up on you, growing in power, taking their time to wear you down until they are strong enough to act in the most devastating way.

What's more, demons don't usually want to destroy their host's body – they want amalgamation incarnation; to take the body over, remove the human soul and claim that body's place on Earth. Without the vessel intact, it would be impossible to do.

Unless what was inside of Julian had far greater power than a regular demon, with such strength that it was instantly too overwhelming... Something that did not need a mortal body, or did not want one...

But Oscar had never known of such a demon.

He made his tea and leant against the kitchen side, trying to quiet his wandering mind, sipping every time his thoughts posed another persistent interrogative.

There were so many unanswered questions, and normally they would pursue and demand answers. But, as it was, they did not have the time or the resources. They were fighting a war that was greater than them, and no one had recognised that more than Julian.

Oscar downed his tea and placed his mug in the sink, next to a draining board of dry crockery.

He decided to make a start on the spare bedroom. He walked in to find it in just as bad a state as the living room was. He began moving boxes, opening them and sorting them into his piles.

Then something caught his eye.

A box, hidden, out of the way, in the foot-space of the desk; as if intentionally out of reach.

What about this box made Oscar so curious, he did not know. He pulled it out and stared at the words written upon it in bold, capitalised marker pen:

Mission Resurgence.

Oscar opened the box to find dusty, browned pages organised into three thick folders. Atop these folders were more labels, written in marker pens.

The first read *Istvan's Journal Extracts.*

The second, *Derek's Journal Extracts.*

And the third, *Julian's Journal Extracts*.

Oscar stared at them, even more unanswered questions presenting themselves, each question offering potential answers that only provoked more confusion.

For starters – who was Istvan?

Secondly – how long had Julian been writing his own journals, and why hadn't he made this known in case of his death?

And, most oddly – why were there extracts of Derek's journals separated from the rest of Derek's journals?

Derek's journals were organised into chronological order on a bookcase across the room, probably the only organised shelves in the whole flat – yet here were numerous pages, intentionally taken from those journals, and hidden away.

So what was it about these extracts?

He took out the smallest of the three files and placed it on the desk, mulling over the name written on the front.

Istvan.

Julian and Derek had never mentioned an Istvan. Not as far as he could recall, anyway.

A single page marker stuck out from all the pages, attached to a page at the end. On the page was a handwritten note, one that became scruffier and scruffier the further it went on. Oscar sat on the floor, leaning against the desk, and read.

This is the final entry of my journals.

I have filled these pages with my knowledge and expertise, yet this is the page that you will find most useful, whilst also being the most frightening. I write it as a forewarning that, if the world recovers from the mess I have created, that such a mess should be prevented from ever happening again.

I write it in English rather than Hungarian, in hope that a universal language will allow more to read it.

I have, since being young, known that I was paranormally gifted.

I found others like me, and we joined together with the aim of finding a use for these abilities. Working in secret, as we feared the world's lack of understanding, we have worked to rid the world of the demonic influence that threatens the world we inhabit.

At first, there were five of us.

I am the last that remains.

And after writing this letter, there will be no more.

It turns out that, in trying to prevent the world falling into peril, we have inadvertently placed the world in far more danger than we ever thought possible.

The Nazis are spreading their curse across Europe. Every day I stand atop my building in the hiding place I have been fortunate enough to keep and watch as they round up families. Normal people, with families themselves, commit these atrocious acts, murdering people in their masses.

These people are responsible for their actions; do not mistake me in saying that. I do not wish to remove the contribution of man to this horrible world.

But such great evil cannot exist without the influence of Hell.

It was my pursuit of saving another one of us that caused this. A woman with whom I was so desperately in love. A woman who, as I feared, was the first of us to perish.

Now I have unbalanced Heaven and Hell, and allowed demonic influence to wreak havoc across the world.

Demons have become people.

People have become demons.

There is no difference between the two any longer.

And this is my fault.

So I bid goodbye, in hope that, with my presence leaving Earth, I will cause no more danger to it.

Please heed my warning. This is what can happen when you meddle with powers once you follow your heart, instead of your senses.

Good bye, and good luck.

Istvan.

OSCAR STARED AT THE SMUDGED, wrinkled paper as his mind dwelled on this man's predicament.

Millions died following this man's actions.

Was the world about to face the same fate because of his?

He felt guilt stronger than he had before.

He didn't want to read any longer, but he knew he had to. These pages, it seemed, had information he needed.

Information Julian hadn't trusted Oscar enough to share.

He turned to the first marked page in the second file and read the first extract of Derek's journal.

THEN

DEREK KNOCKED ON THE DOOR, WILLING IT TO BE OPENED OUT of hope rather than expectation.

Funny, really. A year or so ago, he'd have been ushered in. Jenny would have made him a cup of tea and they would have spoken eagerly about what they could do to save Eddie.

But now Eddie was gone.

As was Jenny.

The war was over. The world was safe again; for now, at least. Eddie was in Heaven with his sister, and Jenny was at rest.

But that wasn't the way Lacy would see it.

She had been an outsider, in a way. Jenny had been Eddie's childhood best friend. Eddie and Martin had been powerful exorcists. He'd been...well, something. A guide. A teacher. A fool. Pick any of the above. But he had still been integral.

Lacy had only been involved because she was Jenny's girl-friend; together since they were eighteen, and engaged to be married once the law would permit them to.

And that was why Derek expected a less than welcome reception. Of course, you never want to lose someone you love

– but for Derek, his deep involvement with the fight against Hell meant there was a level of understanding. He knew it was for a cause, and he fought for that cause every damn day.

Lacy would have thought it was for nothing.

He knocked again.

Still no answer. He saw the movement of a curtain, so slight he wasn't sure if it was a trick of the mind.

He wasn't going away. He wasn't giving up.

Despite how detached Lacy may have felt, she had still played an important role in saving Derek and Eddie. Her abilities as a nurse came in use when she had to bring Eddie and Derek back from deliberate death; something they had done to gain entry to Hell – a voyage that ultimately led to Eddie's hidden evil coming to fruition.

Perhaps Derek had never realised how wrong it had been to put her through that. Maybe he should have spoken to her about it a little more.

But perhaps and maybe was not productive. There were a lot of things Derek would have done differently, and some things he would have done very much the same – but after it's done, it means nothing, and is not worth such rumination.

He knocked again. He hoped she was still alive, that she was still in there somewhere.

As far as Derek was aware, the hospital hadn't heard from her in months. He'd visited a few days ago, figuring her work was a better place to find her than her home. After all, she couldn't run and hide in her workplace.

But she had already been replaced.

They said that she'd just not turned up to work one day. That their attempts to contact her proved futile, and their persistence in trying to find out if she was okay was deemed pointless. In the end, they'd had to give up and post her a letter of dismissal; one they said she didn't contest.

He knocked on the door again.

He hadn't given up on Martin. He hadn't given up on Jenny. And he damn well hadn't given up on Eddie.

He was not giving up on her, either. Whether she felt like she was a part of The Edward King War or not, she had been, and he owed it to her to help.

He knocked again; this time louder, more persistent.

"Open up, Lacy. I know you're in there."

An obvious shuffle moved behind the door. It didn't open, but he knew she was there.

"Come on, Lacy, I can hear you. Just open the door."

Silence again. He knew she was there, pretending she wasn't.

"Lacy, please, I just want to talk to you."

Still she remained quiet.

"Fine, we'll talk through the door. I need your help."

He hoped there would be a response, and he waited for one, but one did not come.

"We won, Lacy. I know it came at a cost, but we won. But only for now. Hell is always looking for a way, and we know they'll come again."

He sighed. How was he supposed to explain all of this through a thick plank of wood? He was having to shout, and he knew the neighbours would hear him.

"It's not the end of it. Heaven has conceived numerous more, just like Martin. They are called Sensitives. And it's my job to find them and help them, and I need your help in doing that."

Derek thought he could hear a scoff, but he wasn't sure.

"I know you feel I'm responsible for everything. And maybe I do accept some of that responsibility. But Jenny died doing what she thought—"

"Go away!" came a petulant shout, and Derek heard stomps as the owner of the voice marched back inside the house.

"Please, Lacy…"

But it went unheard. She was no longer behind the door. She could no longer hear him.

He knocked on the door once again, but it was a weaker attempt, out of misguided hope more than a belief that she would answer.

He wanted to help her. He wanted her to invite him in so he could explain, and he could show her a path that would give her life meaning.

But she didn't want meaning anymore.

In truth, Derek wasn't sure she ever wanted any part of this.

He looked once more at the window. The curtains didn't budge this time.

Defeated, he turned and trudged away.

NOW

LIKE MOST OF THE SISTERS, MARGARET WAS INCLINED TO RUN and hide. With every step she took through the corridor, she found another nun cowering beneath a table or hiding behind a chair or quivering against a wardrobe.

But she was in charge.

And she couldn't let this diabolical shift in behaviour run riot throughout the orphanage. She had to take control, assume some kind of authority.

But she felt it, just like they all had. Just like none of them admitted.

There had been a shift in power.

And this was undoubtedly the result.

She paused beside the kitchen. Little Tommy sat with his back to her, on the floor, rocking back and forth, eating something. Cereal boxes lay scattered, ripped and torn around him, as did their contents.

"Thomas?" she feebly inquired.

No reaction.

But she was not afraid. She would not let herself be afraid, as much as she wanted to be.

This was Tommy.

Tommy who, when he arrived, did not speak for almost eight weeks.

Tommy who, just the other day, drew her a picture of them walking together through a field on a bright summer's day.

Tommy who, just as they all craved, had found a couple that had fallen in love with him and were days away from completing the adoption process.

She had to realise – this was just a child. The same child who had picked her flowers and beamed with excitement at the prospect of a new home.

"Thomas," she repeated. "Can you turn around please?"

She took a step forward, more warily than she would care to admit. She was inches away and she could hear him munching, ravenous chewing, crunches of what she assumed was dry cereal.

Which was odd, as Tommy couldn't stand dry cereal.

"Thomas, I'm not going to ask you again."

She moved toward him. If she crouched and reached her arm out, she could probably touch him, but she didn't.

"Thomas, come on."

He made noises as he chewed. A gnarly noise, as if he was enjoying what he was devouring.

She inched closer, and slowly lowered herself into a crouch, reaching her arm out but not touching him, not yet, not just yet.

"Thomas…"

Tommy paused.

"Thomas, can you please–"

But she was interrupted.

Tommy turned around, the shadows highlighting the childish contours of his face. As his face became clearer and her eyes adjusted to the sight before her, she noticed red smears all over his mouth.

She looked to his hands, to what he was eating.

It wasn't cereal.

She screamed, backed up against the wall, staring wildly at the innocent child holding such a thing.

She wondered who it had come from. Whether it had been a nun, or another child.

She didn't want to know.

He dropped it and went to his knees, snarling at her like a wild boar. He crept slowly forward on all fours, staring up at her, licking his lips as if taking in the sight of a delicious meal.

"Thomas..." she whimpered, but no more pleas came out.

How could a child do such a thing?

Then she realised: this was no longer a child.

She turned, and he galloped after her like a wolf sprinting after its prey. She reached the kitchen and slammed the door shut.

She reversed into the hallway, watching the door, waiting for it to open. The movement of shadows at the door's base terrified her even more than the sight of the sickening child.

She turned and halted.

There were more. At least three of them; in the darkness, she couldn't tell. They were growling, but she was uncertain who was making which noise. Shadows moved behind them and she was sure there were more.

She ran, turning and sprinting through the door to a classroom. She slammed the door shut, turned the lock, and backed into it. As soon as she felt ready to avert her eyes from the closed door, she looked around the classroom, exploring every crevasse. It appeared to be empty.

She did the only thing she could think to do.

She took to her knees, placed her hands together, and raised her head to peer above.

"Heavenly Father, please give me mercy," she whispered.

"Please grant me safe passage, please give my sisters their lives, and please save the souls of these wretched children."

She closed her eyes. Prayed with her mind. Forced her thoughts like she was booming them over a grand hall. Beseeched, begged, pleaded.

As she opened her eyes, she noticed the phone in the classroom's corner. Glancing at the door that just began to buckle, she scarpered over to it and dialled the only number she could think of.

On the other end, the Church answered.

They said they were aware of the situation.

They said help was on the way.

They said they were sending the Sensitives.

And she thanked the Lord for his grace and mercy, knowing she only had to hold on that little bit longer.

12

HENRY STOOD IN FRONT OF THE MIRROR, AS HE'D BEEN instructed to; just as a dozen others did, all across what he assumed was once a dance studio.

"I want you to look at your reflection," Oscar commanded. "I want you to feel your determination, your ruthlessness. You are facing a demon and you are more badass than they are – believe it, and it will be so."

Henry wasn't quite sure how to look *badass*. He had never had a day in his life when he would consider himself so. But he tried, snarling his nose and looking at his reflection with leering eyes, only to feel pathetic and self-conscious.

Everyone around him was doing it.

They were all happy to glare at their reflections.

So why was it only him that felt completely ridiculous?

"Now, repeat after me," Oscar spoke, his loud voice echoing around the studio. "Holy Mother of God, holy Virgin of virgins."

"Holy Mother of God, holy Virgin of virgins," repeated the recruits. Henry only mouthed it.

He noticed a girl walk in and stand at the side. He recognised her from the picture April had shown during her lecture – Thea, her name was.

"Louder!" Oscar demanded. "Holy Mother of God, holy Virgin of virgins!"

"Holy Mother of God, holy Virgin of virgins!"

"I don't believe you!" Oscar insisted. "If I don't believe you, then the demon you are exorcising damn well won't believe you. These are the rites; these are the prayers that will compel this demon to free its victim – so you have to believe they are going to work, you have to *know* you are beating this bitch of Hell. Now – again, with more conviction. Holy Mother of God, holy Virgin of virgins!"

"Holy Mother of God, holy Virgin of virgins!"

This time, Henry pushed his voice out of his barely moving lips, a weak response getting lost among the more powerful demands. Everyone looked so angry, so determined, so successful. He looked like a child. A scared, stupid little child who couldn't even muster enough confidence to say a line with meaning.

"Depart, transgressor!" Oscar bellowed. "Depart, seducer, full of lies and cunning !Now you."

"Depart, transgressor! Depart, seducer, full of lies and cunning!"

"I don't believe you! Again!"

"Depart, transgressor! Depart, seducer full of lies and cunning!"

"On your own, from the left. Go."

A young man to Henry's left shouted the words, his voice forceful, powerful even.

"Good," Oscar approved. "Next."

The next person spoke the words, and Henry realised there was just one more person to go before him.

He was going to have to shout these words in front of everyone. Suddenly, he felt like he was on stage in a school play and knew none of his lines. He was barely able to say the words with conviction with everyone else – now, to say them on his own seemed to be the most terrifying task he had ever been assigned.

"Depart, transgressor! Depart, seducer full of lies and cunning!"

"Good. Now you."

He saw Oscar turn to him in the mirror. In fact, he saw everyone look at him in the mirror. The boy to his left, who had just spoken with such volume and such meaning, looked to him expectantly.

He froze up. He opened his mouth but no words came out, just utterings and murmurings of indistinguishable syllables.

"Come on, go!" Oscar urged.

"Depart, transgressor," he answered, in such a quiet voice he struggled to hear it himself.

"Depart, seducer, full of lies and cunning," he went on, trying to force more power to his voice, but failing.

"I don't believe you," Oscar said, his voice the most powerful. "Again!"

"Depart, transgressor," Henry tried again, his voice louder, but still only sounding like he was having a timid conversation. "Seducer full of–"

"No!" Oscar interrupted. He was next to Henry now, speaking low and deliberately in his ear. "This demon is from Hell, slowly killing what is probably a child younger than you. I want you to look into those eyes and I want you to tell that demon exactly what you think of it."

Henry looked into his reflection, peered deeply into his eyes, glaring intently.

He went to speak.

He stuttered.

He closed his eyes and dropped his head.

"I… can't…"

He didn't need to look at Oscar to feel his disappointment.

"Oscar," Thea spoke from the side. "We've got a call. We need to go."

Oscar stared at Henry a moment longer, then addressed the rest.

"Go get some lunch."

Oscar walked over to Thea and they spoke quietly. Everyone shuffled around him, nattering and talking and discussing, until the noise had filtered out of the room and he was still standing there, intent on not looking at his reflection, unsure why he was not moving.

Oscar and Thea finished their heated conversation, and Oscar left. Thea remained, watching Henry, and he wished she would just leave him alone, and wished she wouldn't at the same time.

"Why don't you come?" Thea asked.

"Huh?"

"We are about to perform a mass exorcism. It might be good for you to come, to see what it is we are up against."

Henry felt every hair on his arms stand on end.

Go with them?

Was she insane?

He could barely say a sentence and she wanted to confront him with demons?

Thea stepped toward him, but didn't approach him.

"We are in a rush, so I can't hang around and pester you. I think it would be good for you to see it."

Henry didn't look at her. He looked at his feet and shook his head.

"Henry, isn't it?" Thea asked.

Henry feebly nodded.

"I think you should come."

Henry closed his eyes. Pretended she wasn't there. Willed her to leave.

"Fine," she said, and her footsteps grew faint.

How disappointed his parents would be.

13

THE CAR WAS FILLED WITH A HARMONIOUS TENSION. APRIL WAS grateful that no one spoke. She wished to be alone with her thoughts.

To her right was Oscar. Behind Oscar was Thea, and beside her was Rebecca.

She had been hesitant to invite Rebecca, but they had needed a fourth person, so she'd had to choose one of the recruits who'd stood out. As annoying and forthright as the girl was, her inquisitive mind was at least a sign of intelligence; or so April thought.

Still, glancing in the mirror at Rebecca, she felt a modicum of resentment.

Not at Rebecca for her rude interruption of the painful lecture April had delivered, as irritating as her impudence had been.

It was just...

That seat looked strange when filled by someone other than...

She closed her eyes. Told herself to stop it. It was pathetic. She couldn't just well up every time she thought of him. There were casualties in war, and he had been more prepared for that than anyone else. It was painful, but there was a job to do.

Still, she felt a growing sense of unease. A cautious hesitance she had never felt before.

The last and only time they went to a building full of the demonically possessed to perform a mass exorcism it had resulted in…

No. Stop it.

She looked to Oscar.

What if it was him next?

Please stop torturing yourself…

He must have felt her eyes on him, because he turned momentarily from the road to glance at her and ask, "Are you okay?"

What if she was honest?

No.

How on earth would I be okay?

That is an incredibly stupid question to ask me.

"Yeah," she muttered.

"I guess that was kinda a silly question, huh?"

She allowed a meagre smile. He'd always been able to tell what she was thinking.

He opened his mouth to speak, then didn't. April imagined he was about to offer reassurance that no one would get hurt, that last time was a one-off, that the worst would not happen – but had stopped himself, realising he couldn't promise such a thing.

Instead, he reached a hand across and placed it above her knee and rested it there, smiling at her again. A forceful smile that, if she hadn't known Oscar as well as she did, may have seemed patronising.

"Do you want to talk about it?" he asked.

God, yes.

I want my mind to explode so all of my thoughts can fire every-

where until they are just pieces of loose debris we can pick up and discard together.

I want to cry hysterically in your arms and break down and fall to my knees and show you everything that is going on in my mind.

Yet, as much as she wanted to talk about it, she couldn't think what she'd say.

Nothing spoken would change anything.

No words of reassurance would bring Julian back.

No opening up and sharing her feelings would make them less valid or less real.

And no admittance of weakness would inspire any confidence in Oscar or anyone else.

Oscar had always told her what a strong woman she was. How he loved her because she didn't need him or rely on him. That she kept him because she wanted him, not because she would ever need a man to burst through the door and rescue her.

Except, sometimes, at her very low points, just like anyone else, she secretly wished she could be rescued. That Oscar could reach his hand into her pit of despair, wrap her around his fingers, and pull her out.

"April?" Oscar prompted.

Oh.

Yeah.

I haven't answered.

"No, I'm fine," she said, though they both knew fully well that she wasn't.

"Well, if you ever change your mind, you know where I am," he said, taking his hand back and using it to change gear.

She was grateful, at least, that he did not ask if she was sure she was up for this. He had enough respect not to treat her like a delicate china doll that could be dropped and smashed at any moment.

He pulled up and killed the engine. They could hear the

rumble of screams before they saw anything. As they approached, the fence surrounding the orphanage came into view, along with a mass of police vans that only added to the desperate vision of the building.

April hesitated only a moment, and made sure no one else saw it.

They would surround themselves with salt, like before.

They would tip holy water onto their finger and use it to protect their body, like before.

They would use three candles to form the holy trinity, like before.

And, like before – something could go wrong. They still didn't know what. Hell, they didn't even know if the mass exorcism had contributed to Julian's demise – though there was no other instance she could think of where a demon could have found its way in without them knowing.

With a surge of feigned confidence, she forced her feet forward and kept up with the other three.

An officer ran up to them. Expecting difficulties, they prepared their excuses, but, to their surprise, the police officer did not stop them.

"Oscar?" the officer asked.

Oscar warily nodded. "That's me."

"We've had the phone call from the Church. They say this is your domain now."

Oscar looked to April; a look that said *wow, if the Church is taking control of law enforcement, then things really have gotten dire.*

"We've been told to quarantine the building and then you'll do what you did before – like at St Helen's Psychiatric Unit."

"That's right," Oscar confirmed with an attempt to sound in charge.

Oscar turned to Thea.

"When you're ready."

Thea took a flashlight and crucifix from her bag and strode forward.

Oscar then turned to April.

"Will you show Rebecca what to do?"

April nodded, then felt suddenly afraid. What if her guidance to Rebecca was poor and her candle went out? If her circle broke? If her holy water hadn't been blessed?

"Are you sure?" Oscar asked, as if sensing her hesitance.

"We'll be fine," April said.

But April could get it wrong... A young girl could die... It would be her fault...

Oscar placed a hand on her arm.

"I'll show her; you just get yourself set up," he said.

"It'll be..." She tried to say *fine*, but she couldn't.

Because she knew it was a lie.

"Honestly, let me help."

He gave her a firm kiss on the forehead, whispered, "You got this," smiled, then left her.

With Rebecca.

Leaving her alone.

She watched them go, hoping that she would see him again.

OSCAR WASN'T SURE WHAT WAS MORE RECKLESS – THEA'S overconfidence, April's desperate uneasiness, or Rebecca's naïve arrogance.

Thea, having accomplished what she did at St Helen's, was sauntering through the barricades like she had just won the jackpot on Bingo.

April, having lost her closest friend once, was edging to her corner with the pale face of dread.

Oscar was tempted to point out their potential reckless-ness, which somehow made him chuckle – that would be exactly what Julian would have done. It was Julian who always gave the cynical view on everything, always forcing a scepti-cism that made Oscar want to defend everyone.

Was that now his role?

Was it now up to Oscar to end other's happiness with painful realism?

Was he going to have to fill the space Julian had occupied?

He had automatically started to lead. There was no spoken decision about this, but there didn't have to be; with April deep in her despair, Oscar was the only one left to keep this hopeless mission going.

He finished giving Rebecca her instructions. She nodded and kept repeating, "I got this" – something that made Oscar feel all the more wary. Her arrogance was stronger than her abilities, and he had never thought that to be a good mixture.

Against his better judgement, he left her to her station. He took his space on the other side of the orphanage so that he, Rebecca, and April formed a triangle around the building.

As Thea placed her hand on the front door, Oscar finished spreading the salt around him and lighting the candles.

As he did so, he wondered what it was that Julian had done so wrong when he did this. Whether there was a gap in the salt, a candle unlit, a prayer incorrectly articulated. He wondered whether the same thing would happen to one of them after their presumed success.

Then again, maybe something already had Julian at that point.

Or, maybe there was no good in wondering about this again. He had thought about it so much that every time the thought re-entered his mind, it was accompanied by a drumming headache.

He bowed his head, closed his eyes, and said the words he had said so many times he could recite them without even needing to consult The Rites of Exorcism.

"Holy Mother of God, holy Virgin of virgins. St Michael, St Gabriel, St Raphael."

At the other point of the triangle, April forced the words on the page out through pursed lips. She'd heard Oscar and Julian say them so many times it was strange to hear them coming out of her voice.

"All holy angels and archangels, all holy orders of blessed spirits."

She pictured Julian next to her.

His hand on her back.

His voice soft and reassuring, in the way he only ever spoke to her.

Keep going, he might say. *You can do this.*

"All holy apostles and evangelists, all holy disciples of the Lord, all holy innocents."

I believe in you.

"All holy bishops and confessors, all holy doctors, all holy priests and Levites and all holy monks and hermits."

I promise you won't die like I did.

She faltered.

Willed the false reassurance away.

And continued.

"All holy saints of God, intercede for us."

At the final point of the triangle, Rebecca wondered what the big deal was. She was just reading words. They had all acted like what she was going to do would be ground-breaking, earth-shattering, maybe even life-altering.

All she was doing was reading a sodding prayer.

"From all sin, from Your wrath, from sudden and unprovided death, deliver us, oh Lord."

Just words.

That was all.

And as Oscar said those words with the same meaning he had always said them with, knowing the power they held, he gave his final mental push.

Come on, Thea.

It's up to you now.

THE SCUTTLES IN THE DARKNESS DIDN'T SCARE HER AS MUCH AS they did before.

Yes, they were frightening. But only on an instinctive level. In truth, she felt so full of confidence she could take on anything and anyone.

Their whispers in the silence were tiny in reality, but deafening to her. She could hear the throbbing of evil, could sense the pulse of Hell convulsing her arm, pushing her hairs on end.

A quick scurry before her was accompanied by a childish laugh that had nothing innocent about it whatsoever.

"Come out," Thea commanded. "I'm not afraid of you."

The laughter intensified, mocking her declaration.

She could feel their prayers.

All holy bishops and confessors.

It poured through her like hot liquid gold.

All holy doctors, holy priests and Levites.

She raised her arms into a crucifix and felt the power of Heaven fill her.

All holy saints of God intercede for us.

There was Oscar's voice.

April's voice.

Rebecca's voice.

And a unity that bound them together.

A sudden leap sprang toward her; a child with their blood-shot eyes wide and their smile curled into a sneer. Their roar was deep, croaky, and of multiple beings. It forced itself through the air like it was being thrown, like something was sending it hurtling at her with a horrific pace.

"Stop," said Thea, raising her arm.

The child fell and cowered at her knees.

More came, peering out of doorways, slowly edging into the corridor, crawling toward her; four-legged silhouettes with demonic faces lit only by sparse lights that broke the shadows.

She stiffened her arms and straightened her back, strengthening the crucifix she made with her body.

She grinned.

Those faces that intimidated her so much before were nothing to her now.

"Leave," she demanded.

They didn't falter. They kept approaching.

But that was okay.

They could come all they wanted.

"Leave!" she repeated.

They kept advancing.

That was fine, it was okay.

They could advance.

"Leave, I say!" she persisted.

But they didn't leave.

They kept on coming.

From all evil deliver us, oh Lord.

Their prayer continued, but it did nothing.

"Leave this place!" she continued, but her voice lacked the edge it had a moment ago.

Another leapt toward her. She raised her hand, said, "No," and it fell.

But the rest kept coming.

Their bones shifting in ways they shouldn't shift, their contorted movements appearing all the more sinister in the darkness.

Her arms fell. She broke the shape of the crucifix.

She stared at the many possessed souls leering toward her.

She backed up, rushing toward the exit.

But she couldn't leave.

How could she leave?

She couldn't tell them it didn't work – that she wasn't what they thought she was.

She tried again.

Refocussed.

Listened to their prayers.

From all sin, from your wrath, from sudden and unprovided death.

What did those words even mean?

No, she couldn't think that.

Now wasn't the time for doubt.

She needed conviction.

She faced the oncoming horde.

Raised her arms once more.

Felt the tickle of a tear at the top of her cheek.

"Leave," she said again.

They sped up, so many of them now, crawling on the walls, on the ceiling, like spiders hunting their prey.

"Leave!" she said.

From the snares of the devil, from anger, hatred, and ill will.

"Leave!" she bellowed.

By your mystery of your holy incarnation.

"Leave!"

From everlasting death.

"In His name I command you – *leave!*"

A wave emitted across the corridor and Thea collapsed.

She came around moments later, wiping blood from her nose.

Through the blurs of her hazy eyes, she saw dozens of innocent children looking around, crying and screaming out of fear.

She closed her eyes and dropped her head again, but refused to pass out, willing herself to her feet.

She stumbled, knocking against the wall, but stabilised herself.

It had worked.

But she hadn't been this weakened before.

She couldn't let the others know.

She couldn't tell them what this had taken.

They were expecting her to do this to the entire world – and she had been severely weakened by a single building.

She took a minute.

Coughed up blood and convinced herself she hadn't.

She straightened her back, told herself it was over, and walked out of the orphanage with as much conviction as she could.

16

THEY BURST THROUGH THE FRONT DOOR AMIDST JUBILANT NOISE. April beelined for the kitchen to find the champagne, Thea recollecting boldly to Rebecca what the experience inside the orphanage was like, and Oscar...

Oscar hung back.

Watched the others.

Thought about the millions being tortured and being killed as they celebrated.

Thought about the thousands of other orphanages being tormented into terror.

Thought about what was to come. How Hell hadn't even gotten started yet.

"To Thea!" April said, raising her glass, clinking with Rebecca and Thea as she did. "I don't know how you did it, but you did it again!"

Oscar stood in the doorway, struggling to quite conceive of the image. April, turning from so subdued to so happy. Maybe she needed this. Maybe this was the celebration, the respite, the success she required to help her move on.

Maybe it wasn't even the successful exorcism she was really celebrating, but the relief.

"Oscar, aren't you going to join in?" Thea asked, noticing Oscar loitering in the doorway.

Oscar deliberated as to whether to say anything or not. Whether to announce his thoughts, his feelings. Whether to voice what he really thought.

Then he realised he would later burst out with ugly words if he did not relieve the burden in a calm manner now.

"I guess I just don't see much to celebrate," he admitted.

"What?" Thea exclaimed. "We just exorcised a whole orphanage!"

Oscar looked down. Contemplated. And looked back up, aware of how melancholy he appeared.

"Yes. An orphanage. In a world of chaos."

"Come on, Oscar," said April. "We have to celebrate small victories."

"But that's what this is, isn't it? A small victory. A very small victory."

No one said anything.

"It's great that we have done another building, but in the grand scheme of things it's nothing, isn't it?"

"Oscar–"

"There is a world out there," he asserted, jabbing his finger at the door, "full of orphanages and mental health units and homes and buildings infested with God-knows-what, needing exorcisms."

"So we'll get to them," April spoke weakly.

"How? We have months, if that, until amalgamation incarnation starts to occur and those demons possessing people start taking their bodies for their own, and masses of demons begin to walk the Earth. And we're celebrating one measly building?"

"We did pretty well–"

Oscar marched out of the room, leaving it in stunned silence, and returned moments later with a newspaper that he slammed down on the table.

"Front page, the headline reads Genocide in Mongolia."

Oscar turned the page.

"Mass shooting in Istanbul."

He turned the page again.

"Man sets himself and a mosque on fire in Abu Dhabi."

He turned the pages in quick succession, reading out more headlines as he did.

"Death in Cornwall, mass suicide in Massachusetts, slaughter at school in Tokyo. Suffering after suffering after suffering."

He looked from each of their faces, only just realising he was out of breath.

"This is nothing in the grand scheme. Doing a building a day for the next three months will do nothing to help the rate of progress we need."

"We're trying–" Thea said.

"But it's not good enough! You are supposed to have this great ability, and we've seen it, but we need more. We need you to do it bigger."

"But I – I don't think I can."

"Oscar," April said, reaching a hand out for his arm.

"We need to do more!" Oscar kept going. "We need to go bigger! Or... well, or we're all screwed. The whole world."

"Oscar–"

"You say you're not strong enough, but you *need* to be strong enough. Masses of people are dying. We can't sit here celebrating a few dozen kids, we have to–"

"Oscar!" April said, placing a hand on his shoulder.

His panting subsided. He willed himself to calm down.

"Look, why don't..." April said, trying to find an answer. "Why don't you just go with Julian and you can–"

She stopped.

Looked to Oscar with wavering tears.

She ran upstairs.

Oscar looked to Thea's wounded expression and followed April, only to meet a slammed door.

"April, let me in," he said.

He heard nothing but crying.

"April, come on."

The door remained shut.

"We can't sit around getting caught up over Julian's death anymore. It was tragic, but we need to..."

He dropped his head.

Julian did so much for her, it must be so hard...

But he couldn't keep making excuses for her. He really felt like they were losing this battle and he needed her to help.

"Look, I think I'm onto something. I found some journals in Julian's stuff, and..."

The door handle slowly rotated and the door opened, but only slightly, just enough for Oscar to see a single eye.

"Please let me in," he said. "I want to help. I want to talk through this."

April shook her head. "It hurts."

"I know, let me in."

April dropped her head.

"I think I just want to be on my own for a bit," she said.

"April, please, come on, let me–"

But it was too late.

The door was closed.

He rested his head on it, trying to think of something he could do or say.

But there was nothing.

All he could do was continue trying to find solutions, to find answers, to find a way – and he would do that by returning to the journals.

THEN

17

When the day had begun, Derek hadn't expected much. He'd made a coffee, munched down cereal mixed with fruit, and strolled out for a newspaper. He'd had a fairly fierce house cleansing at the weekend, so he was affording himself a few rare days off.

Then the package arrived.

A package containing what looked to be a mass of leather-bound, handwritten journals.

And it came with a note.

Dear Mr Lansdale,

I know you don't know me, but I know of you. I don't know how I'm supposed to explain all that I need to explain in a measly letter, and to put into words the importance of the journals I have enclosed in this package, but please, let me try.

It was a sorry fate that these journals ended up in my grandmother's hands. They are written by a deplorable man called Istvan. Once this wretched man took his own life, leaving this world to chaos, he had the selfishness to send these to her – a man she had briefly met, and who had mocked her for being inept in her paranormal abilities compared to him.

I imagine these journals were his last attempt at mocking her, for they forced the burden on her sorry shoulders – a burden that I must regretfully now place on yours.

The world was at war. Millions had already died by the time my grandmother learnt the truth. And it had been up to her to clear up his mess – which involved drastic actions on her part.

I will not share these actions within this letter for fear of it being intercepted. I imagine that, once you have read these journals, you will understand the lengths she had to go to in order to redress the balance between Heaven and Hell, and will endeavour to assure that the world is not plunged into such depravity again.

You do not know me, and I do not know you – but I know you have a reputation for helping people, and all of us that know the truth about a world full of demons know what you did in The Edward King War.

And so it is with much apologies that a stranger such as myself should pass this burden of knowledge to you. I imagine it would give you a more thorough explanation as to why the events of The Edward King War occurred, and why it is essential you do not allow it to happen again, in the more extreme sense that is possible.

I apologise again for passing this onto you, Derek. I have not long left to live, and I needed someone with a responsible mind to understand what would need to be done should history ever repeat itself again.

I wish you all the luck.

Kind Regards,
      Charice Thato

THE LETTER HAD VERY MUCH CONFUSED him, but having spent the entire day sweating profusely as he devoured the pages of the accompanying journals, he had begun to understand the reasons for the alarm with which they were sent.

The journals themselves were written by a man called Istvan who, it would appear, took his own life in 1940 – amidst the Second World War.

And, ever since that war, the human race had lived in the knowledge of the great devastation that could be caused by the human race.

It would appear, through Istvan's story, that the human race had been deceived.

Istvan had written, in the only part of his journal that had much clarity, that the acts of evil that occurred during this war were the actions of man – but could never have been committed without a push from a greater evil.

That greater evil, of course, being Hell.

And, ultimately, the devil.

The entity of the purest and fiercest evil that has ever been perceived.

Derek hadn't been able to understand how such evil had been allowed to enter the world and allowed to give mankind such a nudge. Yes, acts of evil occurred every day, but through the bodies of the possessed, and in far smaller acts.

A man murders his wife. An angry teenager shoots his fellow students at school. A terrorist lets off a bomb that kills a handful of people.

All small acts of violence committed by the nudge of a single demon.

But genocide – that would take a push far greater than Derek could conceive.

But he read on.

And he finally came to learn – there was a balance between Heaven and Hell. A balance that was kept by those that Heaven conceived. Such as Martin, the few that had been conceived before, and the many Sensitives that he imagined were being conceived since.

Hell produced Edward King to address that balance.

So, in theory, that balance could be tilted again.

Couldn't it?

And what would happen if it did?

The question made Derek have to sit down. The possibility that something even worse than millions slaughtered shook him so much, his wobbling knees could no longer keep him steady.

And there was another entry.

A single entry, attached to Istvan's, with a label written in the same handwriting as the letter, reading: *my grandmother's final entry before her death.*

Derek read it, then read it again.

And again, just to make sure.

Her grandmother had addressed the balance, but had sacrificed herself in the most perilous of ways to do it. She had found the solution, but it had come at a cost. Something had taken her place on this Earth; something that had been passed down to her daughter and her granddaughter.

Something that was now slowly killing the woman who had sent these journal entries.

It was the same thing that had found its way into Edward King, and had prompted him to murder without care.

Derek finally understood why someone would so desperately need to address the balance should it ever be shifted again.

He finally understood why it was so essential that he found these Sensitives – that they would undoubtedly be the ones to maintain this balance.

He wrote an entry in his journal about this day, detailing what he had found.

And in that entry, he made it very clear and apparent what one would have to do should the balance ever need to be realigned again, in hope that no one would ever have to do it.

And before he wrote those words, he hesitated, the pen shaking.

He steadied it, and wrote:

It is with great regret, and after thorough examination of my research, that I am able to conclude this statement with certainty – the only way one would be able to address a shifted balance is if one was to face the devil in Hell.

NOW

18

Oscar put down Derek's journal with as much dread as Derek must have had writing it.

His first reaction, as equally useless and inevitable as it was, was denial.

Derek had used a single person's account to substantiate his claim. Derek had made an assertion with little to go on. Derek had said something wild and extreme, and there was no way it could be true.

But Oscar didn't believe those claims even as he thought them.

He had known Derek briefly, but he had known of Derek's expertise – and he was painfully aware of how Derek was rarely, if ever, wrong. Derek had helped him when O'Neil had tricked him, had helped Julian learn everything he knew, and had helped defeat the heir of Hell in The Edward King War.

If Derek made such a big claim, he was unlikely to do it without feeling the weight of such words.

Oscar stepped away from the journals and forced himself out of Julian's spare bedroom. He stumbled against the door frame, pausing to allow himself to regain balance. Somehow, he made it to the kitchen, though he wasn't entirely sure how he got there.

He put the kettle on and opened the fridge. As soon as he removed the top off the milk, the rotten smell hit him, making him gag so much he rushed to the sink so it could catch any vomit.

He considered using the milk anyway, but bits were floating around. He emptied the thick sludge down the sink and discarded the carton on a pile of mess already left on the floor.

For the first time in his life, he had his coffee black. He poured some cold water in so he could drink it straight away and he gulped it down in one go.

Hell.

The devil.

How would someone even...

He filled the mug with cold water and gulped that down in one go too, not caring for the remaining loose grains of coffee sticking to the back of his throat.

He had to tell April.

But tell her what?

How could he possibly put this into words?

He had to do a lecture that somehow let the recruits know what was happening and what they were in for.

But why?

They were hardly all going to run down to Hell and do battle with the most powerful evil ever to exist – an evil far stronger than any he had ever confronted, or even witnessed.

He opened the fridge again, hoping there would be a beer.

There was a bottle of honey whiskey.

He hated honey whiskey.

He opened it, poured it into the coffee mug, and drank it down in another long gulp, retching afterwards and shaking his head.

It was disgusting.

No, he had to tell April. He had to say something.

He went to leave, to tell her, to spill his words into her already burdened existence, but fell as soon as his hand left the steadiness of the sink.

He didn't get up.

He remained on his knees, his head in his hands, his fingers seeping between strands of sweaty hair.

Was he going to have to do it?

Was Thea?

Oh, God, is April?

No, it would have to be him.

This mess was because of him.

But then what? Even if he succeeded, he may not make it out and would be condemned to an eternity of the worst torture imaginable.

So then, he wouldn't go.

What then?

What if he didn't let anyone else go either? Kept this knowledge to himself?

They could just accept the fate of the world. They could stand back and admit, hey, this time, maybe it was too much.

They'd won a great many battles.

He'd fought his demon child.

He'd defeated a prison under the entrapment of evil.

He'd risked his and everyone else's life to save April's.

And now, maybe – just maybe – it was time to admit defeat.

The recruits could go home, spend the last few months they may have left with their families. People could be grateful for the lives they have left, for the little time on Earth that remained.

Maybe he could come clean. Tell the world why such horrific actions were occurring more and more every day, only to be labelled a nut and a preacher and an extremist and to be mocked in the tabloids.

And April...

Maybe he could go home and just put his arms around her, hold her close for as long as he could, relish the remainder of time they had left together. Be grateful that they met, that they loved, and that they felt everything they had felt together.

It could just, simply, be time to give up.

But the thought left as quickly as it had arrived.

Oscar knew he wouldn't be giving up.

And he knew where he may well end up going.

It would be the sacrifice of one man for the survival of the billions.

The only thing he had left was to read the remaining journal entries, read the rest of Derek's words and the pages included by Julian, and hope that there was some kind of salvation in there, something that gave him an alternative option.

Something that told him that there could be another way.

19

ONCE AGAIN, HENRY LOITERED AMONG THE CROWD OUTSIDE THE lecture theatre, alone in a crowded hallway. Unable to find a chair, he leaned against the wall, avoiding eye contact with all of those gathered around him in clumps of acquaintances, talking loudly about everything and nothing.

Henry sighed, wishing he'd brought a book or had a phone or something. His parents had never believed in phones, saying they did not want his mind to rot like other teenagers'. They also filtered the books he read with an army-like regimen, ensuring there was no blasphemy or witchcraft.

He missed them, but he didn't miss their ways. He'd always been the odd one out because of them. Maybe they were the reason he was the only person stood in silence, avoiding looks from strangers.

"Hey!"

He felt someone shout across the corridor to his right. Then he felt eyes on him.

"Hey!" repeated the same voice again.

He risked a short glance in their direction.

"Yeah, you!"

He looked at them, weakly, unsure whether they were referring to him.

"Why don't you come over here?" said a girl.

He looked to his left, expecting another person to come bursting down the hallway.

"Yes, you!"

The girl stood up, marched over to Henry, grabbed his hand, and dragged him to where she and a few other people were stood. Henry stared around at them, but they didn't look at him; all except for a boy who separated himself from the others to join Henry and this girl.

"What's your name?" the girl asked, and he instantly recognised her as the person who kept shouting out in the lecture the other day.

"Henry," he said defensively, slightly overwhelmed by this sudden attention.

"Hello, Henry," the girl said. "We thought you might like to talk to someone instead of being stood on your own."

Henry stared at her. He shrugged, not out of indifference, but not knowing what other action to take.

"My name is Rebecca," she said. "And this is Luke."

"All right?" Luke said, offering his hand. Henry quickly realised he was supposed to shake it, and did so.

"Good," he muttered quietly.

"Don't worry, mate," Luke said. "We ain't going to hurt. Just thought you might like some company."

Henry feebly nodded.

"What do you think so far?" Rebecca asked.

Henry didn't know what she was talking about.

"The lectures, the whole demonologist exorcism stuff – what do you think?"

"I don't know," Henry said quietly.

"I know what you mean," Rebecca said, seemingly unperturbed by the staring, quiet nature Henry was so self-consciously aware of. "It's all a bit, I dunno – namby-pamby, isn't it?"

Henry nodded. He had no idea what that meant.

"We're both exorcists, or so we reckon," Luke said. "What are you?"

Henry didn't know what this meant, at first – then he realised they were referring to all the subtypes of Sensitives. Exorcists, conduits, and so forth. He knew the answer, but for some reason, it did not meet his lips.

"I bet you're an exorcist, ain't you?" Rebecca proposed.

Henry nodded.

"That's cool," Rebecca told him.

"Rebecca actually got to go to one of the mass exorcisms the other day," Luke said.

Henry stared wide-eyed at Rebecca.

"Really?" he said.

He couldn't imagine possibly attending one so soon, if ever. He was astounded that she had been able to go.

"We did an orphanage," Rebecca said. "It weren't that great. I had to recite some prayer stuff in a circle of salt and candles, and Thea went in."

Henry felt a little disappointed, and she seemed to pick up on it, as she added, "It was pretty incredible though, the point when you feel it working – when you know Thea had won, and there was like this surge running through me, like a bolt of electricity."

"Wow," Henry said, very aware of how little he was saying.

"Wish I could go to one," Luke said.

"Just got to be noticed," Rebecca said. "Ask all the questions and they respect you, I guess."

The thought of asking a question during a lecture filled Henry with mortifying dread. He imagined he would never have the impudence to interrogate the Sensitives in the way Rebecca had.

He wanted to ask more, but before he'd mustered the confidence, the door to the lecture theatre opened and Oscar peered out.

"In you come," he said, seemingly stern – more so than usual.

"You can sit with us if you want," Rebecca told Henry. He followed her in, hoping that she did not ask lots of questions and draw attention to herself with him sat next to her.

20

OSCAR PEERED OVER THE YOUNG FACES. ENTHUSIASM MIXED with fear mixed with optimism mixed with severe trepidation. He saw every emotion imaginable staring back at him, and he wished he could give them more hope than he was able.

The burden of knowledge allowed him to look at them differently. Rather than innocent kids needing to learn, he saw them as lambs for the slaughter. Soldiers to unwillingly send to the front line with no idea what they were probably about to die for.

"Today," Oscar began, "we are talking about demons."

He paused, clasping his hands together. Somehow, he found himself unconsciously mimicking how he thought Derek would deliver the lecture, as if that would give him more wisdom or authority.

"Of course, demons are what we fight in most cases. Occasionally we have a wayward spirit or the dead who can't move on – but, mostly, we have demons. It is demons who possess bodies, demons whom we exorcise, and demons with whom we do battle each and every day."

Rebecca raised her hand.

"Not right now," Oscar told her blankly, and she lowered it.

He clicked the space bar on the computer, and a few mythical drawings of demons appeared. At the top was Ardat Lili, the first demon he'd fought, and he felt a sense of childish nostalgia come over him.

"It is never just as simple as demons. Some demons are more powerful. Some have too much power; some have too little. We do not know who we are fighting until we have a name. And that is the first thing you must get out of the demon – its name. Knowledge of the name gives you the power, and you know what you are fighting against."

He raised his arm to indicate the image of Ardat Lili.

"This is the first demon I faced. It was a succubus. Is anyone able to tell me what a succubus is?"

Rebecca's hand quickly shot up.

"Yes?"

"A demon who has sex with mortals."

"Good. And why do they do this?"

Rebecca shrugged. "To impregnate them, I guess?"

"Precisely! Or, in Ardat Lili's case, as she is a female demon – to impregnate herself. In fact, she formed a pairing with a demon that was possessing her father. You can imagine the torture this father and daughter were forced through as they were made to take a backseat in their own bodies. Both survived the ordeal, but the father murdered the girl's mother."

He moved to the next slide, where the picture of a demon with three heads, one of a ram, one of a goat, and one of a man, appeared.

"This is Balam. He is one of the princes of Hell. Demons have ranks – and he commands legions of demons. This is the demon that originally took Edward King's cousin at the beginning of The Edward King War. If you do not know what happened in this war, then you have not done the reading you were set."

Oscar ignored a few shifty looks.

"Often, we have a low-rank demon possessing a person, and very occasionally, a higher-rank demon such as a prince. They possess their victim for one purpose – amalgamation incarnation. Which is?"

Rebecca raised her hand again.

"Let's try someone else."

Luke raised his hand.

"Is it when the demon takes over the body, like, completely?"

"Pretty much. It is when the demon removes the soul from the body and takes that person's place on Earth. During possession, the person is still present, but is in the backseat – now they have been thrown out of the car completely."

He clicked to the next slide. Multiple images appeared, all various interpretations of the same creature. Some with bigger horns, some on a throne of skulls, some with fire emanating from its fingers.

"This is the devil."

Oscar allowed a moment for the name to settle.

"The highest-ranked demon – if you can count him as a demon, that is. He is stronger, more powerful, made of pure evil. He was once an angel, as we all know, who fell from Heaven – and has become so powerful, it is believed he may well be able to overthrow humanity entirely."

He locked eyes with a few of the scared faces.

"The devil has never possessed a person on Earth. As far as we know, that is. But we are fairly confident that we would know – whether through feeling or the actions that would occur as a consequence."

Rebecca raised her hand. Oscar sighed, and reluctantly raised his eyebrows.

"Yes?"

"Why?"

"Why what, Rebecca?"

"Why hasn't the devil ever possessed anyone? It doesn't make sense – surely, if he wanted to take this world, he would do it better himself?"

"That's a very good question."

Oscar paused. Allowed himself a moment of reflection, choosing his words carefully, so the articulation of his answer was as clear as it was important. During this brief moment, he exited the slides on the screen and switched the computer off. He found his way to the front of the presenting space, as close to the recruits as he could possibly get, speaking quietly and sincerely.

"No one really knows for sure. But I can hypothesise."

He looked around at the faces all waiting for the answer, all staring wide-eyed at his perceived wisdom.

"Some say his power and propensity for evil is too great, that a mortal body would not be able to handle it, that it would be destroyed before he'd managed to enter it completely. That a human body would break under its force."

Rebecca raised her hand again, though slower this time, more particularly.

"What do you think?" she asked.

Oscar allowed himself another pause for thought.

"I don't buy it," he answered honestly. "Yes, a body would be under a strain, but he is too powerful not to find a way."

He looked down, then back up again. He wondered how far to go with this, how open to be.

But they were waging a war.

He had to be truthful.

"I believe that he is just biding his time. I believe that, when he is ready, when the world is at just the right moment, at breaking point – he will strike. And we will have to do everything within our power to ensure that moment never comes."

Oscar noticed Thea at the back of the theatre.

He held her gaze for a moment, then dismissed them.

He waited to speak to Thea once the lecture had finished and everyone had gone, but it appeared that she had left too. Instead, he was left alone, an empty lecture theatre doing little to reflect the chaos of his mind.

21

THEA ARRIVED HOME TO A SILENT HOUSE. SHE KNEW APRIL WAS in as the door was unlocked, but didn't care to find her. She was grateful for all April had done, but she was not in the mood to confront her desperate grieving. Every conversation seemed to be loaded with despair; even when Julian's name wasn't mentioned, he was there, hovering around her like a permanent blackness wrapping her in its morbid embrace.

She would have a cup of tea.

She was normally a coffee person, but a cup of tea had always been her mum's solution to all of life's problems. *There's nothing a cup of tea won't solve,* she had always said, simplifying the deepest of life's problems with the taste of a warm beverage.

She filled the kettle.

Put it on its stand.

Pressed the button.

It didn't start. Normally, it would light up green on its base, but no green appeared, nor did a click of the button.

She looked all around it, checking the wire, checking it was on its stand properly, checking it was filled enough.

She stepped back, ready to punch the cupboard, ready to throw the damn kettle out of the window and phone her mum, screaming, *fuck your cup of tea!*

She realised that the plug was not switched on. She pressed the switch and the kettle started.

She rested her hands on the side. Bowed her head. Closed her eyes. Scolded herself for getting worked up over something so trivial.

She looked at her phone. A missed call from Oscar. He must have seen her. She thought she'd snuck out unnoticed.

She hadn't wanted to stick around to discuss his lecture.

Really, honestly, she felt a little…

Perturbed.

Intimidated, even.

Somehow very much aware of how much he knew and how little she did.

She had a strong gift, yes, but so what? The accumulated knowledge of Oscar's many years fighting demons gave him an edge her ability couldn't compensate for.

After all, as he so ardently pointed out – her ability was still not good enough.

The kettle boiled.

She filled her mug.

The water didn't change colour. It just filled her mug with a hot transparency.

I forgot the tea bag.

She opened the cupboard, searched for the box of tea bags. She knew where they were, but their location temporarily evaded her. She searched another cupboard, the next, the next, the next, until she eventually returned to the first cupboard and found them hidden behind a stack of mugs.

She paused.

Breathed.

Fought the instinct to throw that box across the room.

What a feeble attempt at anger that would be. To watch a box silently stroke the far wall and witness a few tea bags tumbling out without so much of a crash or a smash.

She put a tea bag in the water.

She added milk.

The water barely changed colour. It did little to dissolve.

She grabbed a teaspoon and dragged the teabag around the mug until finally, eventually, in good time, the water began to turn a light brown.

"Fuck's sake, Thea," she said for no apparent reason.

She stared at the mug without seeing it, and suddenly she was back at the orphanage, shouting *leave* repeatedly to no avail, until luck intervened.

Maybe that was all it had been.

Luck.

St. Helen's was a fluke.

The orphanage was just luck.

They needed her to perform a mass exorcism on something greater than a building, and she could barely do the building with any consistency.

There was no skill to what she had done. She'd just walked into a building of deranged children and shouted *leave* repeatedly.

She decided, unquestionably and conclusively, that she was not who everyone thought she was.

She poured the cup of tea away.

Trudged upstairs.

Lay on her bed.

Willing a nap to arrive that never did.

THEN

22

DEREK FELT SO VERY CLOSE TO DEATH.

Whether that was hyperbole or the truth, he did not know – but all day, every day, he felt his body weaken and weaken, almost like it was fading away and would one day just dissolve into air.

The only breaks from wallowing around his empty house were the intermittent visits from Julian, and occasionally April and Oscar. Since he was saved from the prison by young Oscar, he had felt very much like a spare part – wanting to help, but his illness making him a burden on all those around him.

It was a shame. Oscar had so much potential, yet he wasn't able to contribute as much as he wished to the boy's learning.

He'd known he was ill long before he'd been diagnosed. He'd had this body for over fifty years, and he was able to tell when something was not right with it. The doctors were doing tests and looking for ways to delay the inevitable – but Derek knew that it mattered little.

There wasn't much anyone could do for him anymore.

Derek had lived a life longer than most in his profession

achieved. He was grateful for what he had. Although, it did sometimes feel a little unfair that, after all he had done for the world, society had left him to lie on his stiff mattress, surrounded by the echoes of silence, every day wondering what would kill him first: his boredom, his uselessness, or his own body.

But it was okay. He didn't need the world to know.

His life's task was not a mission anyone would ever be grateful for. It had always been that way.

There was one way, however, that being close to death could prove advantageous.

It allowed him to try something he had yet to allow himself to try.

Istvan's journals came to mind.

As did the words of Charice Thato and her grandmother.

You will have to face the devil in Hell.

It was the kind of line he would expect to hear from a clueless extremist or a raving preacher, or someone who took all of this on faith and had never seen what Derek had seen. But the empirical evidence he had witnessed told him to trust his gut, and his gut told him that this was not a lie.

If the balance between Heaven and Hell ever shifted into Hell's favour – the only way would be to confront the king of evil in his own domain.

He had done so before, of course. Many, many years ago, in the onset of The Edward King War – he had been put close to death and sent into Hell to rescue Eddie. Something had attached itself to Eddie, meaning Eddie had not returned to this world alone, and this had ultimately pushed Eddie to become the devil's heir.

But this situation was, of course, different. Not that going to Hell in those circumstances wasn't difficult and life-threatening, but the circumstances were different.

Eddie had a piece of Hell in him, whether or not they had

fully realised at the time – meaning that he was able to wield powers in Hell that could save both of them.

Derek would have no power in Hell. If anything, he would have less strength and less control over his own body as he did in the mortal world. And there would be no Eddie to save him. He would be at the mercy of demons he'd spent a lifetime fighting.

And Derek knew that, even if he could find a way back, there was a strong possibility he would not return alone.

But Derek had little to lose.

If something tried to latch on, he would cut his ties from this world. He hadn't long left anyway.

He had to see if it was possible.

He *had* to.

Just to know if there was a way, should it ever be necessary.

He would need to be revived, but he did not want to involve Julian. There was no way Julian could know what he was doing. Maybe someday, when Julian searched for answers in his journals, long after Derek was gone, Julian could learn this grave lesson – but for a man who was supposed to set an example, Derek would be doing exactly what he had strictly told Julian never to even consider.

That's why he chose to do it in public.

He sat in the park. It was night-time, so it would be a while until someone found him – meaning he had plenty of time to try what he needed to. But he knew that someone would find his body eventually and call an ambulance to revive him.

He sifted through the pills in his hand; the pills he had stolen from the hospital upon his last check.

Dimethyltryptamine to simulate near-death.

Metoprolol, Toprol XL, Verapamil, and Calan, all used to lower the heart rate – and, if used together in a high dose, could be potentially lethal.

And, finally, a low dose of Midazolam, Haloperidol, and Propofol. All drugs used in acts of euthanasia.

He stared at the dosage in his hand.

Was this stupid?

Yes. Probably.

But he had to know.

I have to know if it can be done...

He had done it before, with Lacy there to revive him, and had only touched the outskirts of Hell.

He had to go beyond that. Go deeper into the depths of the underworld, searching for the devil, who would probably be sat on his throne of skulls, awaiting the impudent fool who dares surrender his life to an eternity of torture on some whimsical errand.

He swallowed them all before he could stop himself.

He lay down on the bench.

The night sky was already spinning.

His body shook with a frantic delicacy. He could see, but he couldn't move.

Foam trickled down his chin.

He tried to close his eyes but the various colours merging above him seemed to entrap him in a translucent haze, a fixed compression of noise only his eyesight could perceive.

The surroundings disappeared, and blackness encompassed him.

He felt nothing.

Saw nothing.

He ceased to be.

He sank further and further into Purgatory.

And there, he spoke.

"Do not grant me passage to Heaven," he commanded.

He was not ready to go there.

"Allow me to fall to Hell."

He swore he saw Eddie.

He saw the fiancée he once had.

Jenny smiled at him.

And then he collapsed into an endless pit, dragged downwards, his outreaching arms watching the faces of those he had loved and lost disappear.

Screeches overcame him.

And a face appeared.

A face he wasn't able to perceive in the first instance. A face he could only witness once his eyes had adjusted. A face that made his brain pound against his skull, like the creature was reaching its fingers into his head and squeezing, pressing, pinching so hard his migraine was about to explode.

Its reddened eyes, its bloody jaw, hooves, fur of black, all glared at him.

He choked on the face of an evil purer than a human mind could suffer.

And he screamed.

And he awoke.

On a bed, sunshine pouring in, a doctor standing over him, his pillow covered in blood and vomit.

He was mortified. Shaking not out of the piercing pain that seized his body, but out of dread, out of pure fear at the sight he had seen.

It was beyond inhuman.

But it wasn't just what it looked like, it was how it felt...

Like he was empty.

Like his life was worthless.

Like he was falling into a swirling pit of misery and there was nothing but despair, just despair; a blackened, dismal, never-ending pit of desolation and hopelessness.

He cried.

The doctor probably thought it was from pain, from relief of being alive – but it wasn't.

It was from the horrors that had inflamed the migraine pumping against his skull with such fevered ferocity.

After Derek had managed to start speaking coherently again, the doctor said that they had no one listed as a next of kin and asked whether there was anyone he could call.

Derek said no. Besides, he wasn't staying.

The doctor insisted he had to, but when you're going to die soon anyway, why waste your final days laying stationary in a hospital bed?

He would go home.

He would sit in his bed and fill in the pages of his journals.

He would share his final thoughts on the subject and leave it.

This had been a stupid, stupid idea.

He had no idea how long he had been out.

But he knew that it was impossible to go face such an evil with a mortal mind.

And he knew that it was something he would never try again.

NOW

23

OSCAR RETURNED HOME AFTER ANOTHER LATE NIGHT IN JULIAN'S spare bedroom, replaying the final excerpts from Derek's journals in his mind. He heard the words in Derek's voice, and understood the burden with which he wrote them – but that did not make them any less disturbing.

The house was still and dark, and he turned the lock quietly so as not to wake April or Thea. He took off his shoes and placed his bag down silently.

He stared at that bag.

It contained the final folder: the excerpts from Julian's journals.

He picked it up again, deciding he did not want to leave it laying around. The thought of April finding such words written by Julian would just complete her misery.

Then Oscar decided he shouldn't have to keep anything from April. They shared everything, and never kept something like this from the other.

Then again, maybe he needed to finish reading them before he shared them.

Maybe it wasn't a good idea to tell April until he learnt what Julian had written, for fear of what April may discover.

He really did not want to read Julian's excerpts, though he knew he must. He could not see how Julian's knowledge – knowledge that he had kept so secret from them – could possibly make things any better.

He knew he had no choice.

He took the bag upstairs and passed the closed door to Thea's room, then the open door to the spare bedroom Julian used to use. The bed was still unmade, last touched on the night Julian had left it to go to the bathroom and end his life.

He could see Julian's body on the floor of the bathroom as if it was still there. A bloody mess. Contorted and inside out. Streaks of red decorating the tiles.

He could still hear April's scream. Could still see her wide eyes that would not avert themselves from the dismembered corpse.

He could still remember trying to speak to her, but knowing she heard none of what he was saying.

He numbed himself to the thought and made his way into his and April's bedroom.

As he opened the door ever so slightly, April's sleeping body came into view. The covers were wrapped tightly around her. She looked still. The most peaceful he'd seen her in a long time.

He placed the bag beside his side of the bed, removed his t-shirt and trousers, and slid into bed next to her. He shuffled closer, until he was just behind her, close enough to wrap an arm around her waist.

He kissed the back of her shoulder, gently enough that it wouldn't disturb her, then rested his forehead in the curve of her neck.

Her breathing was slow and steady.

His arm tightened, and he felt his open palm over her heart, felt it lightly thudding.

He pulled her closer, feeling her body press against his, relishing it. He hadn't been in this kind of proximity with her for what felt like an age. They had always slept with one of their arms around the other – until recently, when April wanted to be left alone.

But now, with April asleep and unable to isolate herself from him, he enjoyed what he had been missing so much.

He could smell her. The mixture of faint perfume and sweat. It felt so good to be able to take her scent in again, to breathe it in, to recognise its warm familiarity.

"I love you," he whispered, gently enough that it would not disturb her sleep but he knew her unconscious mind would hear it.

The same curve of her buttocks against his waist, the same hair falling irritatingly in his face, the same skin under his sensitive touch.

It made him feel like they were first dating again. Like it was how it used to be. Like the days when they would fall asleep in each other's arms after talking all night.

She began to stir, but only a little.

Enough, however, to reach her hand out and push him off of her, accompanied with a groan.

He moved away. She wrapped the duvet back over her shoulder and returned to sleep.

He lay there, staring at the back of her head, not touching her.

Not going anywhere near her.

He desired her so much, wished her hand would realise its mistake and pull him back, would want the closeness to comfort her pain in the way he knew he could.

But she didn't.

She just slept. Away. Apart. Like she had every day for the last few weeks.

Oscar decided he wasn't tired. He stepped out of bed and took his bag downstairs, into the study.

By the light of the lamp he sat, beginning Julian's journals, trying not to think about what had just happened.

He felt devastated. Crushed. Like the one constant in his life, the thing he loved the most, had moved out of reach and he could no longer have it.

He persevered through Julian's words, because, as he kept reminding everyone – they had a job to do.

THEN

24

ANOTHER DAY, ANOTHER POINTLESS EXERCISE IN DESPERATION.

Julian knew they stood no chance.

He watched Oscar mindlessly attempt to repair the damage he had done, but to little avail. Every idea was another backfire. Every action was another failure, and every word was another piece of infuriating nonsense that only incensed Julian further.

He knew it wasn't helpful to hold onto this resentment.

God, he knew it wasn't helpful.

He just couldn't let it go. Oscar was aware of the irreparable death and suffering his actions had caused, and he had admitted that – but where was the wallowing? The grieving? The hopeless whimpers at the genocide occurring across the world because of his selfish, pathetic 'love.'

He saw it in Oscar's eyes when he watched the news, when stories of suffering and mass killings and suicides and torture became all the more frequent and he would look, and Julian would stare at him, *really* stare at him, to see if there was anything there, any pain or awareness over the constant catastrophe.

Oscar would always pause, then move on.

Of course, Julian knew there was little Oscar could do to reprieve himself; if he did spend his time feeling sorry for himself and wallowing in the grief of what he had done, Julian would get annoyed and tell him to deal with it.

But then again, some things are beyond reprieve.

Some things are beyond forgiveness.

And April. The one for whom he cared so deeply and would never wish to lose. This was the only instance Julian was not grateful to Oscar for saving her.

And she saw none of it.

She did not get mad at Oscar for what he had done, and boy, did that make him angrier.

That was why Julian couldn't tell them what he knew.

He had separated the excerpts from Derek's journal and read them and read them and read them until he could recite most of it by heart.

The answer was clear.

Confront the devil in Hell.

But could Oscar be trusted with the responsibility of the truth?

That was why Julian had been so relieved to discover Thea. The girl with the stronger abilities. Maybe she could be the one to go to Hell. Maybe she'd stand a chance.

But she was only seventeen.

She had no personal ties or responsibility. She had no reason to risk her life.

Oscar owed his life to the world.

And that was why it had to be him.

"What are you thinking?" came April's familiar voice.

"Oh, nothing," Julian said. "Just mindless thoughts."

"Thea is upstairs. She is sleeping. It's probably best if we go in the morning, tell her who she is and what this is all about. She'll deal with the shock better after a night's rest."

"Good idea."

April sat in the armchair across from him.

"Where's Oscar?" Julian asked, though he didn't care.

"I think he's having a shower," April answered.

Julian nodded.

"I want to say that you look troubled," April said, "but I don't think I've seen you look any other way for quite a while."

Julian faked a smile.

"I guess it's just become my expression now," Julian said.

"I know there's a lot to be troubled about, but I worry that you are just sitting there, night after night, seething about Oscar."

Julian did not fake a smile this time. He snorted and turned away.

"I'm right, aren't I?"

Julian shrugged.

"The kid has no idea what he's done," Julian declared.

"He does."

"He clearly does not."

"He does, Julian. I assure you, he does."

"He could show it."

"What, to you? The man who's held an eternal grudge against Oscar since the day you met him?"

"I have not held a grudge since–"

"Well whether you have or haven't, he knows what he's done. He doesn't need your constant judgement over it."

Julian's fingers dug into the arms of the chair.

"Thousands have died because of him, and millions more will die yet. And you tell me he doesn't need my judgement? My judgement is the least of his worries!"

"Exactly. And that's why he doesn't need it."

Julian's fingers curled into a tight fist.

"I love him, Julian," April said. "And you need to understand that."

Julian scoffed and turned away.

"I love you dearly, Julian, as a brother, as the person who did everything for me. But I love Oscar with my soul, with the fluttering feeling of my stomach and the warmth of my mind. Every piece of me loves him."

"All right, all right." Julian wasn't ever one for this nonsensical romanticism.

"You just need to know that," April said as she stood up. "Because hopefully that will change the way you keep treating him."

She left the room.

Julian watched her go, her words mulling around like a swarm of locusts infesting his thoughts.

And he understood that his adoration and caring for April was more important than his grudge.

To lose Oscar would kill her.

And that was why, maybe, Oscar shouldn't have to be the one to go.

It would have to be Julian.

NOW

25

A BRIEF SEPARATION FROM THE WORLD OF THE PARANORMAL WAS just what Thea needed. She felt guilty for spending an afternoon away – but an afternoon away would help clear her mind and allow her to return stronger, therefore being more productive to the task.

At least, that's how she kept justifying it to herself.

She lay on the grass, allowing the noises of children playing and friends talking and mothers scolding to meld into the ambience of the park and focussed her energy on her mind, clearing it of all clutter.

But it didn't work.

All those thoughts and worries and concerns about how she couldn't do what they needed her to, that she wasn't good enough, that she did not have the ability to make a huge difference to the world, returned. It was like she'd put up a dam in her mind and the water had seeped through the cracks, then burst it down with little penetration.

A cloud drifted by in the shape of a face, and she could feel those hollow, blue eyes judging her, the indefinable shapes of white puff shaping the leer of its loose visage.

She sat up.

It was no good.

She could just go back.

But oh, how she didn't want to. She wanted to run away, at least for an afternoon, and forget about it all.

Forget about how inferior she felt, all the damn time.

She was still young, still learning about life, and they treated her like she was something so much greater, with all their hopes and yearnings for the world to be saved pressed down on her, pressing so hard she was sinking further and further into the ground, and they kept pulling her out just to tell her to do better.

She closed her eyes. Dropped her head. Interlocked her fingers in the strands of her hair.

Someone was staring at her.

She looked to her left. Across the park. A child. A boy, young and grubby, glaring.

His mother's attention was fixed to her phone, as if it was more important than supervising her child.

Thea stared back.

The kid didn't look right.

His face was growing pale, his eyes were dilating more and more, his arms shaking.

Finally, he caught the mother's attention.

She spoke to him. Thea assumed she said his name, though they were too far away from her to make it out.

He didn't divert his attention.

His gaze remained fixed.

The mother looked up and saw Thea. She looked embarrassed. She said his name again. She even pulled on his arm a little, tried to move his face.

His chin remained rigid, his neck stiffened in place, his eyes unmoved.

He hadn't blinked.

The whole time, he hadn't blinked.

"Stop it!" the mother snapped, loud enough now that Thea could hear.

Thea could see behind this child's mask, see the entity bursting against his fragile skin, the evil within.

This child was another of the many who had succumbed to evil.

Thea wondered how long the child had left before he was ripped of his body.

"Listen to me!" the mother continued. "Stop it!"

The mother looked to Thea.

"I'm so sorry," she announced.

"It's fine," Thea lied.

The boy's mouth curved into a grin that looked out of place on a child.

"Whatever are you doing?" the mother continued, growing more and more frantic.

Then the child's lips opened, and it spoke in the most gravely sinister way a child's voice could, and even though he spoke quietly, Thea could make out every word.

"You aren't what they think you are," it said, flatly and smugly.

"Stop it!" the mother continued.

The kid didn't. Its lecherous grin persisted.

"You are going to let them down, and it will be your fault."

"Stop it!" The mother turned to Thea again. "I really am ever so sorry."

"You are going to let them down, and you are going to die, and they are going to die, and it will all be because of you."

"Right, we're going!"

The mother stood, dragging the boy up by his arm. The boy's face didn't move. The mother tried pulling him away, grabbing his head and turning it around, but his head resisted with a strength the mother didn't expect.

"Don't say I didn't warn you."

"I really am sorry; I don't know what's got into him."

"Their deaths are on *you*."

The mother dragged the boy away, fighting against his resistance, until he was removed from view.

He kept his eyes on Thea until the very last moment.

THE TOOTHBRUSH PASSED ALONG APRIL'S TEETH WITH LITTLE speed. Her gums ached under the lightest pressure, and April knew she should press harder because of it, but didn't want to feel the pain.

She spat blood and continued lightly brushing.

Avoiding her reflection, she spat her final mouthful of blood and rinsed her toothbrush. She took a swig of mouthwash straight from the bottle, held it in her mouth for a few seconds, and let it go.

The house shook under the weight of the front door opening and closing. The front door left little to subtlety, allowing no one to walk in unnoticed.

As the stomps up the stairs grew heavier, April left the bathroom.

Thea trudged toward her room without looking back.

"Hi," April offered.

Thea's grim face turned and gave the smallest of smiles as she continued to her room.

"Are you okay?" April asked.

Thea hesitated, her hand resting on the door handle. She

seemed to stare at her hand. Her body fell loosely, her stance drooping, and her weight falling to her calves.

"Fine," Thea said, entered her room, and shut the door too quickly for April to respond.

April wondered whether she should knock on the door, whether she should persist. But it wasn't as if she could say or do anything, so she walked downstairs.

Oscar sat at the kitchen table. A folder lay before him, but his eyes were closed.

She watched him for a moment.

Considered waking him.

Talking to him.

Telling him everything.

Breaking down the barrier and allowing all the pain and loss to come out, to use all the words she had prepared but never said, to unleash the beastly rant her anguish desired to let out of its cage.

But she didn't.

She just watched him.

She wasn't sure how long it was, but eventually his head rose, and his tired eyes widened in recognition.

"Hey," he said, quickly closing the folder.

"Hey," she replied.

"How are you?" he asked.

She hesitated, then said, "Fine."

He looked disappointed with this answer. Like he was expecting something better.

He must look forward to the day she answered with a different word than *fine*.

"I was wondering," she said, about to offer her heart, her soul, an opportunity for them to spend some time together and for her to tell him everything.

"Yeah?" he prompted.

She hesitated again.

"Nothing," she said.

That look of disappointment met his face again. His shoulders, which had been tensed, dropped.

"Are you sure?" he asked.

April nodded.

No, I'm not.

This shouldn't be so hard.

She should be able to talk to him.

He should be the one that made things better.

"I'll get back to this, then," Oscar said, reopening the folder, his hopeful smile fading to a pained frown.

"What is it?" she asked.

"Just some reading that might help us," he answered without looking up.

She watched him a moment more.

She opened her mouth to speak.

"Osc–" she managed, but she did not complete his name, and had not been loud enough to draw his attention.

He was already absorbed in his reading.

With a last glance she left him to it and found her way to the living room, where she sat in silence for the rest of the evening.

2 7

THE BOY'S DEMENTED GLARE REMAINED IMPRINTED ON THE forefront of Thea's thoughts.

Somehow, it had known everything she was thinking.

It had used it.

And the mother, clueless as to what was happening, assumed she was raising a delinquent...

A light tap on her door and she held her breath, fearing making any sound that may make someone think she was awake enough to talk.

She did not want to see anyone.

Especially April and Oscar. The two who had believed in her. They'd sat in that morning's lecture, placing such faith in her to deliver a talk on what she'd done.

Then the questions came.

How did you do it?

Why did you do it?

How come you can do these things?

She tried to answer.

At first, she was successful.

Then her body grew stiff, her eyes darted from expectant face to expectant face; wide, naïve eyes looking to her for answers.

She was a seventeen-year-old who'd been in this for weeks.

How was she supposed to answer these questions?

What actually is a demon?

What physical properties do they have?

How do they manifest?

She didn't quite realise how little she knew until the bombardment of questions came, inquisitive minds firing thoughts like bullets.

Oscar had stepped in.

Answered a few questions, then ended the lecture.

She hadn't wanted to talk to them.

It was like she was laying at the bottom of a quarry and the rocks kept tumbling over her, one thing after another: the difficulty of the orphanage, the stress of the lecture, and the boy…

How had that boy known?

He had known everything.

Not just who she was, what she was doing, but how she was feeling about it. Her thoughts, her troubles, her desperate insecurities.

And the worst thing…

That boy was right.

She was going to let everyone down.

She was going to get it wrong at the vital moment.

She was going to die or get someone else killed.

The taps on the door ended, and a few steps shuffled away.

In a decisive moment, Thea stood. Strode to the phone. Picked it up.

Hovered her finger over the number.

If she did this, she couldn't undo it.

What with how difficult it had been to begin with…

She remembered how life had been before she found the Sensitives. The constant voices, the chasing faces, evil being a constant voyeur.

Everyone thought she was crazy, including herself.

She was going to end everything.

Then they came…

And what has she done?

Become a burden.

A let-down.

She was not what they thought she was.

She closed her eyes and, with her face scrunched up, dialled the number.

After a few rings, her mother's voice answered.

"Hello?"

She hesitated. She could still hang up and her mother wouldn't know it was her.

"Mum?" she said, taken aback by how small her voice came out.

"Thea?" Her mum sounded so relieved, so eager, almost instantly out of breath.

"Mum…I want to come home," Thea said.

"Oh, Thea, yes. Yes! Where shall we get you?"

She couldn't let them come to the house. She didn't want them to know where Oscar and April were. She wasn't sure why, but it didn't feel right; what if her mum came in and confronted them or something?

No, there was a petrol station a ten-minute walk away. They'd meet there.

She gave her mum the directions and hung up to constant repetitions of, "I love you, dear, I love you, I love you so much."

She opened her door with the slightest creak.

All the bedroom doors were closed. Except the spare room where Julian had stayed, but no one ever went in there.

She crept to the stairs and out the front door, closing it with as little thud as she could manage.

With her bag over her shoulder, she began the longest ten-minute walk of her life, glancing back at the house only once.

THEN

WHY WAS IT THAT EVERY TIME JULIAN HAD TO MEET SOMEONE for information, they were always located in some twisted, bizarre dwelling?

He stepped out of his car and paused. He rechecked the directions the nurse had given him – this was it. The house she visited three times a day to take care of an incontinent old man – the man who, in her words, *makes me feel all kind of chills.*

According to this nurse, this man shouldn't be left alone in a house with just visitations. He should be kept in a home or a secure hospital. But, as she said, strictly "between you and me" – no one wanted to accommodate him. Such people are better left so far back in one's memory that they eventually fall out.

A garden path paved his route beneath a wooden archway. Julian imagined that, once upon a time, this wooden archway would have been home to multicoloured flowers, bright leaves, and branches with delightfully fresh fruit. Now, everything was overgrown and dying. Dead roots clung to the wood like string around turkey. What few leaves were left were brown and crunchy, and the pavement was covered in weeds and nettles.

A deep breath and he began the walk, stepping each step as if he was heading to the gallows. He stepped over what he thought were the remains of a dead bird – couldn't be sure; it had been opened up and picked at by other animals so much that it was barely distinguishable from any other discarded carcass.

He reached the front door.

He could turn back.

He could easily just spin around and power-walk back to his car, turn the ignition, and leave.

He could just abandon this whole idea.

He didn't need to speak to this person.

In all probability, it would only make his task all the more daunting.

No.

I have to.

I must.

If he was to save Oscar from his burden, he was going to have to plunge his own soul into Hell. To do so, he was going to need to know what he was getting himself in for.

And that was why he had to meet the only living man who had spent a prolonged time in Hell and returned – even if that meant confronting what may become his own fate should he come out of this alive.

He placed three heavy, evenly spaced knocks on the thick wooden door.

Nothing.

He wondered if he could hear the shuffling, but it was probably just the wind.

He knocked again. Another three heavy, evenly spaced knocks.

Upon another silence, he placed his hand on the door knob, only to find that the door just creaked open of its own accord.

Before him was a hallway of shadows. Elegantly executed

architecture created a path of doom, old furniture creating a sinister image.

He stepped forward. Choked on a mouthful of dust. Felt the floorboards sink and moan beneath his feet.

"Mr Sears?" he called out.

Nothing.

He took another step, sure that he heard a squeak and a scuttle from behind him.

"Mr Sears, are you there?"

A sudden succession of footsteps pounded across the upstairs hallway.

Julian really did not want to go upstairs. He was hoping to find the man in the living room, sitting casually, awaiting a civil conversation.

He reached the bottom step. A stained carpet stuck up, ripped and torn, revealing the dark-brown wooden slabs beneath it. Placing his hand in his pocket and clutching his crucifix, he began his ascension up the stairs.

"Mr Sears?" he asked again.

Every step was another groan, the staircase singing his voyage to the top step.

"Mr Sears, can I speak with you?"

A bang and scuffle came from a room across the hallway. The door was open, but Julian could see nothing. Every window was covered in black sugar paper, giving only a few sparse shafts of light.

He edged toward the room.

"Mr Sears, my name is Julian Barth. I would like to speak with you."

A shadow moved within the room.

He reached the doorway and peered in.

He saw no one, at first.

But a movement from the far corner attracted his attention, and he could make out the indeterminate lines of a human huddled in the corner.

"Mr Sears?"

He could turn back now.

He could run down those noisy steps and out of the front door and never look back.

No. I have to do this.

He stepped into the room.

"Mr Sears, my name is Julian Barth. Would I be able to talk with you?"

Two bloodshot eyes grew wider, a mixture of brown, white, and red abruptly visible. They stared at him without saying a word.

"Mr Sears, if I could–"

Julian leapt back as Mr Sears pounced upwards. Mr Sears, however, did not come toward Julian – he crawled on all fours to the opposite wall, where he took his chalk and began drawing.

He was whispering something, and Julian strained to make it out.

Mr Sears suddenly stopped and stared at Julian, then resumed drawing. There were all kinds of drawings. Some Julian recognised as poor imitations of demons he knew of. Some were ritual signs. Across all of these drawings was a tally with a great many numbers counted.

"Mr Sears, what is this tally for?" Julian asked.

Mr Sears did not reply. He just kept muttering.

Then he stopped again, turned to Julian, stared, then resumed.

Julian stepped forward.

It was at this point he realised that Mr Sears was drawing him. A poor imitation, yes, but the frequent breaks to capture the image that Mr Sears kept taking, and the representation of exact contours of his clothes, and the poor reflection of his hair, made it clear.

Julian took another step forward, his fingers hurting under the strain of the crucifix's edge pressing hard into his skin.

"Mr Sears, why are you drawing me?"

Mr Sears began a low chuckle, then muttered to himself, this time a little louder.

"He doesn't know, he doesn't know, he asks me why I draw him and he thinks he can be helped and he doesn't know doesn't know doesn't know he doesn't doesn't doesn't know..."

"What don't I know, Mr Sears?"

A large *hah* burst out of Mr Sears's mouth.

"He wants to go to Hell wants to go on a holiday on a trip on a journey take a bag now take a bag don't want to forget your galoshes."

"Mr Sears, how do you know I intend to go to Hell?"

Mr Sears's drawing became more and more frantic, producing the picture with more vigour and more recklessness. What was originally a fairly accurate imitation was now becoming a messy, childish drawing of a man Julian could no longer recognise.

"Mr Sears, how do you know I–"

"Come to ask me questions he has he has he has come to ask me questions like that will help him like anything can help him the balance of the world is off it is it is it is the balance of the world is off and he wants to go to Hell to fix it but he doesn't know he doesn't know by George he does not know."

"What don't I know?"

The man's arm ceased drawing so abruptly it was as if he had been paused and frozen.

The white chalk dropped and clattered.

Mr Sears picked up another chalk.

A red chalk.

His head slowly rotated toward Julian, and he locked eyes and stared as he began drawing with the red chalk.

In fact, he was not drawing at all.

He was scribbling over his drawing of Julian until it was completely covered in red – keeping his eyes on Julian's without a single blink.

"Mr Sears, what is it I don't know?"

Mr Sears's mouth grew into a large grin, a grin too big for a person to form.

Julian regretted coming here.

He readied himself to leave.

But Mr Sears got to his knees, kept grinning at Julian, and waved him closer.

Julian hesitated.

"Tell me from here," he said.

Mr Sears shook his head and waved Julian closer again.

"Please, Mr Sears, just tell me from here."

Mr Sears shook his head more determinedly and waved Julian closer once more.

Julian edged closer, keeping a foot hanging back, ready to escape at any time.

Mr Sears waved him closer still.

Julian edged further, close enough now that he could smell the acrid garlic upon his putrid breath.

Mr Sears whispered something.

Julian, unable to hear it, moved his ear inches from Mr Sears' mouth.

And then he heard it.

"The devil is going to eat your soul for breakfast."

Mr Sears leapt at Julian. He stumbled back, out of reach, then turned and sprinted for the stairs.

He could hear the mad cackling gaining on him as he ran.

He did not stop panting until he pulled the car up outside his house a little over an hour later.

NOW

29

HAVING LEARNT ALL THAT HE HAD LEARNT OVER THE LAST FEW weeks, one could forgive Henry for the alarm he felt when hearing a tap against his door at 2.00 a.m.

He sat up and stared at it, remaining motionless, idle, waiting for the noise's next move.

Another tap again. Maybe it was a tree branch.

A tree branch indoors?

His tired mind struggled to adjust.

He sought the crucifix Oscar had encouraged all of them to have ready at night. He had said that they were all targets and that they should prepare themselves as such, ready to defend themselves from any attacker.

Although, Oscar had also said that the power of the crucifix was only as strong as the belief of he who held it; which meant that a crucifix in Henry's hands would have very little power.

The tap came again, this time with a hushed voice.

"Henry."

His body stiffened.

"Henry, it's Rebecca. Wake up, you stupid sod."

His body relaxed. Not that he wanted to be disturbed during the night by people, but it was a lot better than being disturbed by the dead or demons.

He pushed himself from his bed and dashed to the door, very aware that he was wearing Star Wars pyjamas. He opened the door just enough for them to see his face and not his garments.

Rebecca was there, fully dressed, with a woolly hat and her hair pulled back into a ponytail. Luke was also there, stood eagerly behind her.

"What?" he asked, deliberately rubbing his eyes to show how tired and disinterested he was.

"Get some clothes on, we're going on a trip."

"A trip?"

Oscar hadn't warned them about a trip.

"Yeah, we're sneaking out."

No, no, no, no, no.

Henry was not the sneaking out type.

He was the sit in the background, obey the rules and do not get noticed type.

Every part of his mind screamed at him not to go.

"I can't," he said, though he knew his disposition was so monumentally feeble that a little more peer pressure and he'd do anything to avoid confrontation.

"Come on, mate," Luke insisted.

Henry shook his head.

"I just want to go to bed," he said.

"Look," Rebecca said, putting a hand on his door so that he could not close it. "Aren't you fed up of all this theory? Of asking all these questions that don't get answered?"

On the contrary, you're the one asking all the questions...

"I know it's scary, but I went on a mass exorcism and I didn't even see anything."

That was true.

She did go on a mass exorcism with the Sensitives.

Maybe she would be a good person to explore this with. Maybe she would be able to keep them safe.

"I want convincing," she went on. "So does Luke. And, honestly, so do you. We're going to go confront one of these things and find out if it's actually real, or whether it's a crock of shit made up by a bunch of whack jobs. Now, you in or not?"

Henry hesitated.

He wanted to know. He wanted to see it for himself.

But he naturally did not want to be part of any risk.

"I'm not giving you a choice," Rebecca decided. "Get changed. If you're not out here in two minutes, I'm barging down the door."

Henry nodded and closed the door.

He looked to his pile of clothes at the foot of the bed.

She wasn't giving him a choice.

He may as well appease her.

He would find out the truth, at least.

He reappeared outside within the two-minute time constraint, dressed and ready to go.

Rebecca grinned, seemingly delighted he was coming, as did Luke.

"So where are we going?" Henry asked.

"We saw a message to Oscar, it come up as an alert on the screen during his lecture. Someone needs help."

"I wrote down the address," Luke added.

"What if it's—"

"Oh, come on!" interrupted Rebecca. "We weren't brought here for what-ifs."

She turned and charged down the hallway. With an excited smile, Luke followed.

Henry looked back at the door to his bedroom.

The door to safety.

The door to his bed, where he had been protected and warm only minutes ago.

Ending his hovering glance, he turned and followed the others, ignoring the lurching feeling in the pit of his stomach.

30

THE PETROL STATION WAS CLOSED AND THE ROAD WAS EMPTY. The darkness seemed to wrap its hand around Thea's throat and squeeze, constricting her breath until she choked.

She had all kinds of wrong feelings.

A burning anger in her belly. A fiery resentment mixed with a frozen rage.

She had no idea whether she was doing the right or the wrong thing.

She wasn't even sure right or wrong existed anymore.

The word *evil* was a man-made word that they attached to Hell. She was positive that the devil did not parade around the underworld, chuffed at how 'evil' he was.

Maybe she was going to have to concede Hell winning.

A familiar people carrier pulled up beside her and the window rolled down. Her mum's teary face stared back at her.

Thea saw how much this had destroyed her mum.

She had left and wounded her mum, and the pain she had caused had all been for nothing.

She opened the door and looked at the seat where a packet of *Space Invaders* awaited her.

"It's your favourite," her mum said, as if Thea didn't know.

Thea forced a smile and sat down. Her mum's arms wrapped tightly around her and Thea let them, and she said nothing.

"I missed you," her mum said. "We missed you."

"I missed you too," Thea said. And she had. She had given little thought to what she had left behind – but now, in this moment, she realised how much she was lacking something without her mum there.

She looked down at the crisps left lovingly for her. She readied her hands to open them, but never did. She just held them.

She hadn't had these crisps for a long time. They had been her favourite, but when she was fourteen. She wasn't sure what her favourite was anymore.

"You not going to eat them?" her mum asked.

"I'm not that hungry," Thea said.

"Is everything okay? Did they hurt you?"

"God, no." Noticing her mum's expectant stare, she added, "Honestly, no. They were really great people. I just...I'm not so sure if I'm great too."

"Oh, darling, of course you are!"

Funny, isn't it?

How a mother can have little to no understanding of what is being spoken about, yet find a way to be reassuring about it.

She wondered if she should be honest, and whether her mum would be as reassuring then.

"You know," her mum began, "I'm sure school would take you back. If I spoke to the head of the college, and you agreed to make up for what you missed of your studies, then I've no doubt they will be welcoming. You were always such a good student, promised A's all round."

Thea didn't answer. This was a lot, and it was all very soon. And she wasn't sure if it was what she wanted.

"And the hospital would be willing to start treating you again."

"What?" Thea snapped. She hadn't expected this. She'd explained things to her; her mum should know she was not sick.

"If you want to resume treatment for your... problem... then the hospital would undoubtedly be willing to—"

"What problem, Mum?"

"Well, you know..."

"No, I don't. What problem?"

Thea held her mum's gaze, beginning to understand that this was a mistake.

"Well, you don't honestly believe... I mean, I know that you told us, but..."

"But you think I was lying?"

"No, dear, of course not. I mean, I believe that you believe it."

Thea suddenly regretted everything.

Oscar and April had understood. Had taught her.

Her mum had only doubted her.

"Look, I'm just grateful that you're coming home."

Home.

Thea considered the word.

Home.

"It's no good running away from things, is it?"

Thea let those words settle, let them impress upon her mind like a fist in sand.

"No, Mum," Thea said. "You're right."

She stepped out of the car.

"Thea!"

"I'll come back, Mum. Someday."

"Thea, please."

"Really, I will. The day you start to trust me, I'll come back. Until then..."

Until then, I have a fight to be part of.

She turned and walked.

Paused.

Turned back, her mum reaching out for her from the driver's seat.

She hadn't even bothered to get out of the car.

"I love you, Mum," Thea said. "Goodbye."

She marched back to the house quicker than she had left it, feeling full of resolve, determined, a renewed sense of purpose and vigour powering her stride. She returned home, ready to do whatever she could.

She had been so close to making the wrong decision.

She was lucky her mother had made her see sense.

But her reinvigorated resolve was halted as she was taken aback by the sight of a boy on her doorstep.

As she grew closer, she recognised him as one of the recruits.

She remembered talking to him, offering him an opportunity to join her on the exorcism at the orphanage.

He had refused.

Henry, his name was.

As she stepped toward him, she could see his body convulsing with tears. He was in despair, speaking words that did not make sense, crying helplessly with no end to his hysteria.

"Calm down," Thea insisted. "Hey, calm."

He finally stopped talking, but the tears did not falter.

"What's going on?"

"Dead..." he whimpered.

"What?"

"Dead... both of them... they are dead..."

31

THE THREE OF THEM HAD BEGUN THE NIGHT CONFIDENTLY
enough. Even Henry was close to believing they were going to
charge into the room and rid the body of its demon, their
confidence was so infectious.

"Good evening, madam," Rebecca addressed the bedraggled
woman opening the front door. "I apologise for this late hour,
but we are here to help."

"Who are you?" the woman asked quietly and cautiously.

"Your son, Thomas, is in trouble, I understand?"

The woman continued to glare at them.

"We have been sent by Oscar," Rebecca said, her lies so
convincing Henry wondered whether Oscar had in fact sent
her. "We are here to perform an exorcism on your son."

The woman's grim expression instantly turned. The bags
beneath her eyes grew a lighter grey and her frown morphed
into a pained smile.

"Please, come in, come in," she insisted; and, with a smirk at
the others, Rebecca followed the woman in.

Henry held back a little, allowing Luke to go ahead. The

house was cold, and welcomed him with a cruel sense of fore-boding he couldn't quite articulate.

"No, thank you," Rebecca said to the offer of a cup of tea. "We would like to get to work straight away. Where is the boy?"

Henry continued to look around at pictures of a happy mother and happy son coated in shadows, child's toys left strewn across the carpet like helpless captives, DVD cases of children's films left open and empty upon broken tufts of carpet.

Everything that was positive came with a sense of dread. Everything that was loving was sad. And everything about the place told Henry they should turn and go.

"Guys," he went to say, but was cut off by the others moving briskly upstairs. Henry glanced at the mother's face of hope as he followed them.

The bedroom they aimed for was directly in front of the top step. White light seemed to seep from the crack beneath the door, yet, when they entered, there seemed to be no light at all.

On the bed, bound by wrists and ankles just like in every cliched horror film Henry had seen, was the boy. Thomas. Seven years old.

He didn't look to be in pain. He didn't look to be suffering or wriggling in torment. He just looked like a child, asleep and taken prisoner in his own bedroom.

How could a person do this to a living being? How could a person knowingly tie a child to a bed?

He began to decide who he thought the real evil ones were.

"Have you got a crucifix?" Rebecca asked.

Luke shrugged. She looked at Henry.

"No," he answered.

"How the hell are we supposed to do this without a cross?"

"I dunno," Luke answered.

"What else did they say we needed? Like, the rosary stuff that goes around your neck and the Rites of Exorcism – you got any of those?"

"I don't know, Becca, you were the one who dragged me out of bed and took us here. I thought you might have it."

"Shit," she said. "We'll have to try and remember the rites then, and hope we don't need the other stuff."

She turned to the boy. Sweet, with ruffled ginger hair and pyjamas soaked in urine.

"Strange," she mused.

"What?" Luke said.

"He doesn't look all that bad," Rebecca said. "I thought they'd look different. Like, I dunno, have acne and scars and stuff. He just looks like a kid."

Luke looked over the boy. He stepped forward, placed his hand on the kid's forehead.

"He's freezing," Luke observed.

"He's probably ill," Henry said. "He's lying in his own wee."

Rebecca looked to the others.

"I don't know, guys…" she said.

"What?" Luke asked.

"He looks like he's being abused to me. He doesn't look like he needs an exorcism… Maybe we should call social services?"

"We can't do that!"

"Why not? Just look at him."

"Hello?" came a feeble voice from the bed.

Rebecca rushed to the boy's side.

"Thomas," she said. "Are you okay?"

"Who are you?" he said, his voice so weak. Maybe too weak.

"My name is Rebecca. I'm here to help you. Has your mum been hurting you?"

He looked to the others, then back to Rebecca.

"Yes," he answered. "She's been hurting me."

"What has she been doing?"

"She tied me to the bed and beat me. She said I couldn't go to the toilet, that I had to go here, and then she laughed at me. Then she took my clothes off and…"

He turned his head and closed his eyes.

"Guys," Rebecca said, suddenly urgently. "We can't leave him here."

"What are you thinking?"

"Let's take him and call the police. We can't leave him with his mum; look at what she's done to him!"

Henry watched the boy. He was very forthright for a child so young. He thought that abuse victims typically took a while to admit what had been done, that a child so young would not be able to articulate such atrocities so well.

And the boy's face… It looked in pain, but it also looked a little smug.

"The knot's too tight," Rebecca said, trying to work her way through the rope around Thomas's wrists.

Luke took over and, pulling until he went red, he loosened one wrist, then started to work on the other.

"I don't know," Henry said, still looking at the boy.

"What?" Rebecca snapped.

"It seems…"

What? It seems what?

"Don't you want to help me?" the boy asked, his voice so sad, so meek.

"I don't know," Henry said again.

The other two ignored him and carried on working through the restraints. Within the same second that Luke had released the other wrist, he was suffocating. His eyes bulged from his head and he batted at the boy's hand, but the strength of the child was too much.

"Stop!" Rebecca shouted. "What are you doing? Stop!"

The boy turned and grinned.

His face didn't seem so childlike anymore. His pupils grew,

his skin reddening, his throat throbbing like bumps were crawling inside of it.

Rebecca looked at the door, but it shut of its own accord. Henry ran to it and tried to turn the door knob, but it wouldn't open. It had no lock; it would just, somehow, not open.

Luke gasped and spluttered, furiously punching at the boy's arm, beating at it with all he had, but his strength was diminishing.

"Help!" Rebecca screamed, rushing to the door and beating against it, knocking Henry out of the way so she could pull on it some more.

Luke's face emptied. His body fell limp.

The boy kept going.

As if it knew.

As if it had knowledge of how death works – that the body falls unconscious before it dies, and he would have to wait just a little longer.

And, once the boy had finished, he dropped Luke to the floor like a bag of rice, a smatter of blood trickling from his mouth.

The boy's body rose. His feet stayed tied to the bed, but his body straightened ninety degrees, until he was parallel with the wall.

"Please!" Rebecca begged. "Please!"

The boy's hand stretched out toward the bedroom window. It imploded, and the glass smashed into thousands of pieces, but didn't move from the window frame. It hovered. Then, as the boy swiped his hand toward Rebecca, the broken glass flew across the room and nestled its mass of tiny shards into her skin.

The boy slashed his hand upwards. A large mark spread across Rebecca's throat and she could no longer scream. Blood gurgled down her wounded chin. She fell limply to the floor, just as Luke had done.

Henry's instinct took over his terrified mind. Whilst his feet would barely move under the strength of his fear, his desire for survival coerced them to sprint.

And sprint he did, finding his way to the window and jumping out, the branches of a tree breaking his fall.

He ran and did not look back.

32

THEA PLACED A CUP OF TEA BEFORE HENRY AND HE JUST STARED at it.

She was being nicer than he expected, and more gracious than he deserved.

He sat in silence, the walls of the kitchen closing in on him, the solidity of the chair aching his thighs.

Thea leant against the kitchen sink, a hand on her chin, considering the story.

"What am I going to tell Rebecca's parents?" she asked. "Luke's parents?"

Henry shrugged.

He felt like saying, *this was Rebecca's idea, she did it all; she forced me to go.*

But he didn't.

He did not want to sound anymore childlike than he felt.

He just kept quiet, sure that was the best thing to do.

Thea huffed, dropped her head, and rubbed her eyes. He could see her struggling to know what to do or say. It was almost five in the morning; it had been a long night, and the aftermath was far from over.

"I suppose I don't have to point out how incredibly stupid this was?" Thea said, her voice strengthening. "How you put yourself at risk, as well those that…"

He was glad she couldn't bring herself to say it.

He wished she would, but he was glad, nonetheless.

"I just…can't believe…"

Neither could he.

It hadn't quite dawned upon him yet what he had witnessed.

He knew now that demons were real, that they were dangerous, and that they were waging a war.

But he wasn't quite sure he was responsible enough to handle that information, let alone be responsible for the loss of someone's daughter and someone's son.

"I'll pay for a taxi," she said.

"I can walk–"

"Think I'd trust you to walk home, do you? No. Besides, it's not safe for you. That thing may have followed and just be waiting for you to be alone."

That thing may have followed.

The only words that could have made this entire ordeal worse.

"Just be glad that Oscar isn't here."

"Really, Thea, I didn't want to go, Rebecca–"

"I don't want to hear it. This was a reckless, pointless loss of life. There will be funerals, repercussions… how do you think the other recruits will feel about the job they have to do now? You think they'll stick around? No, Henry, I have heard quite enough."

Thea had met Rebecca. They all had. They knew how stubborn and inquisitive she was. Thea must know, deep down, that this wasn't his fault.

At the same time, Henry couldn't blame her for taking her anger out on him.

A car pulled up outside.

"Don't tell anyone," Thea said. "We don't want to cause a panic until we've decided what to do. Now get out of my sight."

Henry left the untouched cup of tea and trudged out of the house and into the taxi. He stared catatonically out of the window, watching the world go by and seeing none of it.

He wondered if his parents would welcome him back after being so excited to see him leave.

He wondered if he even wanted to go back.

Whether he wanted to stay.

Or whether he was just a lost boy without a place in the world.

33

"I TAKE IT YOU HEARD?" THEA SAID, WATCHING OSCAR WATCH Henry leave out the window.

"I rarely sleep anymore," Oscar said. "And there was quite a commotion."

"Shall we alert the families?"

Oscar sighed. Sat on the bottom step. Leant his head against the wall.

Thea sat down next to him.

They allowed a peaceful moment of silence to go by without either saying anything about it.

"I can't believe I'm going to say this," Oscar softly announced, making sure not to wake April, "but I wish Julian was here."

Thea smiled.

"He'd know what to do," Oscar added. "And he'd be good at playing the bad guy. I don't want to have to tell this girl's parents…"

He ran his hands through his hair.

"I'll do it," Thea reluctantly offered.

"No," Oscar refuted. "It has to be me."

"Julian did say there would be casualties in war."

"Yeah, but not pointless ones like this. Are we not keeping good enough track of them? Should we be there with them?"

"We can't be there all the time. We're responsible for their safety, but if they choose to be foolish…"

"Two kids have died, Thea."

"I know."

Oscar stood. Ran his hands through his hair.

"We're losing, Thea," he said. "We've made progress, but if we continue at the same rate of progress, then we don't stand a chance."

"We'll try new things."

"No. I've been doing some reading. I think I'm starting to learn what I have to do…"

Oscar peered upstairs, aware that April could be listening, and led Thea into the living room. Once they were in, he shut the door and spoke to her in a hushed, hasty voice.

"The Church hasn't a clue," Oscar said. "They think an army of Sensitives is what will win this war, so that's what they sent us. But all we've got are a bunch of arrogant kids who don't know what they are doing. We've learnt that."

"They will learn."

"But not in time." He looked at Thea. So young, yet so responsible. He thought about himself at her age, what a loser he was, how immature he had been compared to her. "I think we need to send them all home."

"What!"

Oscar turned and walked toward the window, not quite sure why. He peered out at nearby houses, all the lights out. People hours away from waking up for work, no idea how little time they probably had left in this world.

"We've just started training them, and you want to send them away?" Thea demanded, walking after him.

"We've learnt tonight that they are only burdens. It's not going to help us."

"Then what!"

Oscar looked at her. Held a deep breath, then let it go.

"I've been reading Derek's journals. And Julian's journals."

"Julian kept journals?"

"It would appear so. They both seem to say the same thing."

"What?"

He looked to the door, as if expecting April to emerge, and lowered his voice again.

"It's extreme," Oscar said. "The solution is extreme. But it may be the only way."

"Yes, what is it?"

"I want to be sure before I say anything. But this could be our shot."

"Then tell me! I need to know!"

Oscar went to leave, and paused in the doorway.

"Send the kids home. Then we'll talk."

"I think it's a really bad–"

"I know, Thea," Oscar said as he left the room. "Send them home."

THEN

3 4

JULIAN WATCHED SILENTLY, KNOWING HOW STANDOFFISH HE seemed, how obviously still resentful of Oscar.

They could think that all they want.

But he wasn't resentful for what Oscar had done anymore, but rather, resentful as to what he was going to have do on his behalf. What he was going to do to protect him, for April's sake.

He couldn't imagine what they'd say if they heard what he had planned.

So he listened as they deliberated over the ins and outs and particulars and events of the mass exorcism of St Helen's Psychiatric Unit.

Julian believed this could work. Though he also was aware it may not.

He was also pertinently aware that it didn't matter.

They'd do it to show their strength and for them to gain some faith in their abilities, but Julian knew it would never be enough.

So, during a pause in discussions he stepped out, and found his way to his car. His hand somehow turned the key, the ignition announced the starting of the engine, and he steered off the drive.

He couldn't do what he had planned alone.

He'd do it without the others, knowing he may not return, knowing it could be his death sentence, knowing that they would likely try and stop him and volunteer in his place. They would know once he was done. If he was successful, they would celebrate his glory. If he wasn't, they would commiserate his death.

But this woman was the only one who had done this before, with Derek and Edward King – and she was the only one who had brought them back. Albeit, with severe repercussions of Eddie becoming the heir to Hell, and under circumstances where Eddie's innate links to Hell allowed them an easier return – but she had still done it.

That was why he needed someone who understood from experience – someone who would know that the best idea may be to not bring Julian back.

In all honesty, he didn't expect to return from Hell. Survival probably wasn't an option. And he wondered why he wasn't so resistant to the idea of death. He wasn't sad or suicidal – he just didn't see what the big deal was about living.

About forty minutes or so after starting the engine, he pulled up and killed it. He knew which house it was straight away and wondered when the day would come that he didn't visit someone with a dead, overgrown garden and closed curtains.

He stepped out of the car and walked determinedly up the cracks of the pavements, ignoring the hiss of a cat perched atop a cracked bird-bath.

He rang the doorbell.

There was no answer, but there was also no sound. Assuming it wasn't working, he knocked on the door instead.

No answer.

He knocked louder, hoping to convey his persistence through his fist.

Still no answer.

The twitch of a curtain caught his attention, but there was no movement when he looked.

"Lacy, I know you are in there!" he shouted.

The cat hissed at him again.

Julian had never particularly been a cat person. He didn't mind dogs – but would never have kept one in his home. The only pet he ever had was a lizard named Fred his parents bought him when he was six, and it died little over a year later.

"Lacy, I'm not going anywhere until you answer this door!"

He stepped back. Surveyed the house. There was no other way in. The windows weren't just shut, they were bolted. Through the grass and weeds that went up to his knees was a side door, but he assumed that was reinforced too.

"I'm here because you know Derek!"

He waited, hearing nothing but silence.

Fine, I'll have to do this outside.

"In case you don't know, Derek died. It wasn't anything supernatural, it was a terminal illness."

The curtains didn't move. No flicker of movement came from the house.

But he knew she was in there.

"It was years ago, but I don't know if you knew. It might be good for you to know that not everyone had Eddie's fate."

He sighed. This wasn't working.

"Derek cared deeply for you, and I know you helped him, just as I know you know what I want to do. Derek visited you before, I know that, and he…"

What?

He what?

What could he possibly say?

The cat hissed again.

That fucking cat.

Julian felt like picking the cat up and throwing it across the garden.

Not that he'd dare touch it with the hissing. Ridiculous, really – he could take on horrific demons sent by Hell, yet he was too scared to put his hand on a damn hissing cat.

"Please, Lacy."

Nothing.

He dropped his head.

"I'm begging you," he said, though it was so quiet he wasn't sure he heard her. He wasn't one to audibly grovel.

Defeated, he backed away, keeping his eyes on the house. He paused at the end of the path.

"You know I won't be the last, don't you?" he added. "You can ignore me, but more will come in the future. This is a fight you can't help but be a part of."

He wondered if he saw the curtain twitch again, but it was probably just his hopeful imagination.

He returned to the car and readied himself to drive back to April and Oscar's.

But he didn't drive back.

He knew he had to try this first.

Even if it meant doing it alone.

NOW

HENRY AWOKE TO NEWS HE WASN'T EXPECTING, BUT DIDN'T surprise him. The corridors were filled with gossip and confusion, people asking questions and speculating answers.

"...they've told us all to go home..."

"...apparently there was a death..."

"...oh yeah, I knew her, she was right gobby..."

Henry was shocked that he did not want to go home. As heavy as the memory of the previous night was, he did not want to return to his parents and answer their questions.

Why did they send them home?

You did what?

Oh, Henry, we are so disappointed...

He couldn't face them. He truly couldn't.

But Rebecca... Luke...

The sight of a body full of energy, consumed with passion, desperate to succeed, suddenly so limp... So full, then so empty... Like a rag doll come to life and then...

The bloody marks across the wall behind Rebecca's slit throat.

Maybe she was still alive.

He ran before he could tell.

But she wasn't.

He knew she wasn't.

He made his way through the corridor, fed up of listening to all the hearsay, and walked into the kitchen, where he poured himself a glass of water.

A few others were gathered around a television. He went to leave, but was instantly distracted by Rebecca and Luke's faces on the screen.

"The first, Rebecca Fern, and the second, Luke McFarlan. Seventeen and eighteen, respectively, found slaughtered in this woman's house. The boy, who was tied to the bed in the room where the bodies were found, had marks all over his body. We are yet to discover what exactly happened in this house last night, but we can undoubtedly speculate."

The sight of the boy with towel around his shoulders and a police officer at his side, leaving the house, hobbling and hunched over, alarmed Henry with a heavy sense of guilt.

Should he say something?

Should Oscar? April?

"There's an update," one of the people watching it said, taking out his phone. "They have released a statement. It was suicide."

"We all know it wasn't suicide," said another. "The Church is covering it up."

The Church is covering it up...

Can they do that?

Henry meandered to the window, hoping for a respite in the world outside. Cars pulled up and students poured into them – some reluctant, some too eager.

He bowed his head.

This is all my fault.

Where would he go now?

He had no money, yet he desperately did not want to return to his parents.

He would go to Oscar and April.

Plead his case.

Tell them they shouldn't punish everyone else because of him.

He wished he hadn't gone.

He wished he'd just gone back to bed.

He wished the scene from the previous night didn't keep replaying over and over in his mind.

He wished he could get some sleep.

But, most of all, he wished he could just shut his mind off from everything for just one moment.

Without enough money for a taxi, he was going to have to walk. It could take him hours.

But what the hell else was he going to do?

Maybe if he kept moving, he would stop seeing their dead, helpless bodies.

He packed his bag and set off, ignoring the hushed whispers of those he passed.

"No way."

It was exactly the reaction Oscar expected after sitting April and Thea down and telling them what he had learnt.

"Not a chance," April continued. "Nuh uh, not doing it."

"April–"

"Don't even try and talk me into it! It is not happening."

She stood and marched from the living room. The sound of the garden door opening and slamming shut was the only thing to end the silence between Oscar and Thea.

Slowly, Oscar raised his head and looked to Thea. She didn't look back.

"It's the only way," Oscar said.

"I thought I was the only way," Thea said.

"You will be needed. Essential, even." He took a step toward her. "Who knows how much the balance will be shifted again when I'm gone. You'll be needed here to fight off anything that occurs in my absence."

"I just – how would you even do it? It sounds ludicrous."

"Basically, I'd be put as close to death as possible without me actually dying, slowing my heart, my breathing – and when I enter Purgatory, I deny my route to Heaven, and... well..."

Thea shook her head.

"I was wrong. It doesn't sound ludicrous – it *is* ludicrous."

"I know."

"I mean – what if you die?"

"It might happen."

"What if you are trapped in Hell forever?"

"Again, might happen."

"What if you come back, but bring something else with you?"

Oscar sighed. Why was he trying to convince her? She knew little of this world, as strong as her power was; the real person he needed to convince was outside.

Not that he needed to convince her to let him do it; that decision was already made. He just needed her to be there to help.

He needed her to be able to make the big decisions that may need to be made.

Leaving Thea to her rigorous head shaking and blinking of disbelief, he walked to the garden.

He paused for a moment, looking at April. Stood alone. Face in her hands, back to the house.

She was so damn beautiful.

So headstrong.

The definition of a strong woman.

The most commanding woman he knew. A woman who did not need him but kept him around anyway.

But he had shown a few too many times that he loved her too much. That he had neglected decision for fear of hurting her, or because she may not like the outcome.

This was the moment he no could longer make selfish decisions. This was the moment he finally had to do what was right and ignore what it was he wanted.

He was going to have to be as strong as she was – something he knew he was not.

"Hey," he said, stepping out. He remained by the door.

She didn't answer.

"You know I'm doing this, with or without your help," he said. "But with your help, we stand a much better chance of things going well."

"Shut up, Oscar," she said, and he could hear crying in her voice.

He strode toward her and put an arm around her. She didn't push him away, but she didn't step into his embrace, either. She stayed idly still.

"The idea of it is stupid," she said. "You know that, right?"

"If I thought I had any other choice–"

She waved her hand and turned away.

"April, you have to be willing to–"

"Stop it, Oscar. Just stop it."

Her stubbornness was something he loved about her – but right now, it was not helping.

For once, he was going to choose the fate of the world over her.

He was going to make the decision he should have made all those months ago.

"I'm doing this, April," he said, his voice low and determined.

"Oscar…" She turned toward him, her cheeks red and her eyes lost. "I lost Julian. I am not losing you too."

Oscar knew he'd regret his answer before he said it, but also knew if he didn't say it, he'd regret leaving his thoughts unsaid.

"But you *are* losing me."

She frowned, tears morphing into fury.

Oscar didn't stop himself. He had to say this.

"You've barely touched me since it happened. I try putting

my arm around you, and I get nothing. I may not be dying, April – but *we* are."

She stared at him.

He wondered what she was thinking. What was going on behind those eyes?

For the first time since they'd met, he felt like he didn't know her.

Like they were strangers who had never met.

"Fine," she said. "Do what you damn well please."She walked back inside the house.

Oscar did not follow.

THEN

This was a stupid idea.

A very, very stupid idea.

But, like most stupid ideas, Julian did not realise it was stupid before it was too late.

He'd sedated himself, used the same drugs as Derek had specified in his journal to slow his heart down, and had now left his body attached to a stolen IV kit from the basement of the nearest hospital.

He'd reached Purgatory, where his route to Heaven had been laid out for him. It was an attractive route, paved with lights and gold, joyous laughter enticing and the voices of those he had lost and loved calling him forward.

It had taken all the strength he had to pull himself away and deny his own entry.

When he opened his eyes he was on a bumpy rock, surrounded by lava that lashed over the side, singeing his shoes. He felt light and heavy at the same time. Like he was a non-existential being, but the burden of his sins gathered in his body and made every movement strenuous.

Screams decorated the distance, screeches of pain and hollers of anguish. It was all he could hear.

But he could see no one.

Just more mounds of stone, yet none of them having as much of a lashing as the lava around his. He was stuck in the centre of its small circumference.

He stood, feigning confidence, knowing he had already failed.

"I am here to speak to the devil!" he screamed, and his throat hurt more than it should, like razor blades digging into his skin.

"I said I am here to speak to the devil, grant me passage!"

A booming laughter reverberated behind the screams. He wished he had thought this through, that he had considered what to do or say when he arrived. He had been so focussed on how to get here that he had no idea what to do now he had succeeded.

"I said I am here to—"

His insides twisted into agony as if something fiery-hot had been rammed between his cheeks and forced through his intestines and into his bowels. He fell to his knees under the force of the pain, wiping sweat from his brow and failing to resist tears.

The pain stopped, and he had a moment to regain his senses, to regain his mind. He had to think clearly, no matter what was done to him, no matter what was—

Another sting punched down his throat and into his lungs, spreading like wild-fire, soaring around his non-existent body like snapping locusts chewing on his breath.

He coughed, bringing up a mouthful of blood that surrounded a beetle as large as his fist, and it splattered over the stone.

An eternity of torture had begun, and he already struggled against the first minute.

"I said," he repeated, striking his voice with confidence even he didn't believe, "that I am here to see the devil."

A being presented itself, a fiery tail behind a well-built torso, legs of muscle, and multiple heads of multiple animals – Julian saw a bull and a goat before the agony started again. The demon raised its fist, and this seemed to spark another burst of fire up his anus, spreading to his chest.

"The devil?" its voice boomed, followed by raucous laughter. "You are not fit for his audience."

"Please," Julian begged, knowing this would only satisfy the demon more. "I am here to–"

Julian's whole body spread out, stiffening, every cell and spread of skin and tinge of muscle and softening bone filled with raging anguish. He sweated and cried and pleaded and despaired, but it all just led to more satisfaction in the many faces of the wretched beast hovering before him.

"We will allow you out of here," the demon said, smug, grinning. "But for one purpose."

Another sting of pain and Julian's eyes opened.

He sat up, panting, wiping his brow.

He felt for his arms.

His legs.

His face.

It was intact. He was here. He was alive.

Had it even been real?

He was back.

Thank God, he was back.

He didn't care how, but he had returned well enough to realise it was a foolish task.

He needed to get to his journal, to document, to warn anyone else in the years to come who may try such a thing.

But he wasn't able to get to his journal.

He wasn't able to direct his feet to his flat or the pen to his hand.

Because he had been granted passage back to his realm, not by the mercy of the demon, but by the plotting.

He was back.

But he was not alone.

NOW

3 8

April put down the final journal.

Finally, she understood what Oscar had been reading.

Finally, she understood why he was so adamant about this.

And finally, she understood why she would be unable to stop him.

But she'd still try.

Footsteps arrived from outside the living room. She recognised those footsteps as Oscar's. Odd, really, how you can come to know someone so well you know what the sound of their step is like.

She walked into the hallway to find him heading toward the front door.

"Where are you going?" April asked. "You're not going to do this alone, are you?"

Oscar looked at her for what felt like a long time.

"If I have to."

"I really wish…"

She wanted to say, *I really wish you weren't so dead set on doing this.*

But, if she was going to make a wish, it would be for him to go back in time and let her die so that the world could live. If he had made the tougher choice she may not be here, but they would not have had this predicament.

In fact, if she was really making wishes, it would be to go back in time before that and prevent him from leaving to find his answers, prevent herself from spawning a demon child that caused such pain, and go back to a time when it was just them, battling together, falling madly in love and not caring who knew it.

But, unfortunately, her wishes were rarely answered.

"I'm going to find a woman," Oscar said. "Her name is Lacy. I assume you read about her?"

"Yes."

"And I assume you read the rest of the journals?"

"...Yes."

He took a step toward her. He didn't touch her, but he was close enough to.

"So you understand why I have no choice."

"Why does it have to be you?"

"Who else?"

"I don't know!"

"Thea needs to stay here and face any consequences."

"Consequences?"

"Yes. We may be seen as weakened, and we don't know what they will send, and Thea is the only one who can take on an army."

"An army? You think they'll send an army?"

"I don't know what they will do, April!" April wasn't sure why Oscar was shouting. "Do you think I have a clue what I'm doing? That I'm not making this up as I go along? I am just trying to do my damned best, instead of moping around!"

He remained poised for an argument, then the tension fell from his body and he looked to the ground.

Was that the first time he'd ever shouted at her?

"I'm not moping around," she said.

Oscar scoffed.

"It's been really difficult–"

"It's been difficult?" Oscar snapped. "How do you think it's been having to do the work of three Sensitives at once? You think it's been easy learning that I am going to have to–"

He turned away and marched toward the door. She knew she should let him go, that the conversation was not productive, that arguing wasn't going to change anything, but she did not want to see him walk out that door like this.

"Oscar!" she cried.

"What?" he barked.

"I – I'm scared."

He shook his head.

"So am I, April."

He left.

She watched the door shut behind him and watched it stay closed for a good while after that.

Somehow, she knew that they had probably shared their last *I love you* and their last kiss and their last moment of sincere affection.

They were doing this today, and there was nothing she could do to stop that.

And she knew she was about to lose him.

39

OSCAR PERSISTED IN KNOCKING ON THE DOOR, NOT TAKING NO for an answer. He'd stay there all day if he had to. He noticed the curtain twitch; he knew she was there.

"Lacy, I am not leaving!"

He banged on the door continuously, knocking and knocking with a heavy fist. The door shook as he banged with more vigour, refusing to stop.

"My arm will get tired before you do!"

It must have been almost twenty minutes of banging until the door swung open and he could finally drop his tired fist.

"Go away!" she barked.

Oscar put his foot in the way of the door to prevent her from swinging it shut.

"I'm not going anywhere," Oscar insisted. "Not unless you are coming with me."

"I am not going anywhere with you; I just want to be left alone!"

The sight of her was something to behold. Her hair was matted into a greasy mess sticking in all directions, her skin clung to her bones like cling film wrapped around meat, and the aroma of body odour wafted out of the house with every swing of her arm.

"But you can't be left alone," Oscar said. "You live in a world with people in desperate need of help and you know this."

"I don't care!"

Her voice was croaky and harsh. He wondered when the last time she used it was.

"You've seen the news, I'm sure. You must know how many people are dying. It's because of an imbalance between Heaven and Hell."

"And what, you plan to go to Hell to redress the balance?" she said mockingly.

"Precisely," Oscar answered, keeping his stony face straight and empty.

She shook her head.

"You're crazy."

She tried to close the door again, but he didn't let her.

"With all due respect, Lacy – you're living alone in a house surrounded by weeds and grass. If either one of us is crazy, it ain't me."

She leant forward, narrowed her eyes, intensifying her glare, and spat each syllable with spite.

"Get. The. Fuck. Off. My. Lawn."

"No," Oscar said, staying strong. He wasn't going, he knew that. He'd camp between the long strands of grass if he had to.

"Why won't you just go!" she said, her stubborn voice now a long, drawn-out moan.

"You must have known that one of us was eventually going to knock on your door."

She refused to answer.

"I need your help."

"To do what?"

"To send me to Hell."

She stood back, shaking her head and folding her arms.

"I know it's asking a lot."

"Why me?"

"Because you're the only person who's done it before. You sent Derek there, and you were able to bring him back, and bring Eddie back too."

"And you know what came back with Eddie? What it did? How it hurt—"

She cut herself off, not able to say the name of the woman she loved.

Oscar suddenly felt sympathy for her. He wondered, should he had saved the world instead of April, whether he would have ended up with a similar fate to this wretched woman.

"You can't hide from this," Oscar said, trying to sound calmer, like he understood, like he was finally reasoning with her.

"Another boy came a few weeks ago, you know. One like you."

"That boy would have been Julian."

"Well, you are a lot more convincing than him! Next time, tell him not to come."

"There won't be a next time, I'm afraid. Julian is dead."

She huffed, closed her eyes, dropped her head.

"And that's why you shouldn't do this," she said solemnly. "Don't you see? How many more of you have to die before you give it up?"

"Every last one of us, if that's what it takes. But if this works..." He took a step toward her, into the house. She flinched back, but didn't run. "I'll be doing this, with or without you. But I stand a far greater chance with you. You have a duty to do this."

"No I do not!"

"But you do. Everything this world holds dear relies on this."

He stepped forward. This time, she did not flinch.

"What would Jenny do?"

"Don't you use–"

"I've read about her. Jenny. She sounded brave."

"Yeah, and where is she now?"

"Probably in Heaven with her oldest friend, looking down at you and wishing you would stop living like this."

He huffed. Looked around the house. The wallpaper hung off, the paint cracked, and there wasn't a single photo frame in sight.

"Please," Oscar said.

Her eyes dropped.

"We'd need to stop at the hospital for some things," she said quietly.

Oscar grinned, but only for a moment. This was one small victory in a mass of trials – but it gave him just that little bit more chance of survival.

THEN

40

JULIAN COULD TELL SOMETHING WAS WRONG.

It was not something he could articulate – and, even if he could, something was stopping him. The whole drive to St Helen's he watched the others, glancing from one face to another, wanting to say something.

Something's wrong with me.

I'm endangering the mission.

I really don't think we should do this.

But it was as if something was covering his mouth, stifling any sound, quelling any resistance, suffocating him any time he tried to speak.

He was being watched.

All the time.

At least that's what it felt like.

Like someone was peering over his every movement, like a headmaster or a police officer but nastier, ready to scold him for doing anything wrong.

Guys, I need help... Please help me...

He said the words, but they didn't come out.

He screamed them in his mind only to find his helpless thoughts squeezed into a tight fist, then squashed and squished like bad fruit.

They pulled up.

He'd been himself at the house only an hour earlier, able to speak his mind, protest and argue, but that seemed like years ago now, and he felt himself being pushed further and further away, almost watching his body as it moved.

Then it all seemed to change. He seemed to be in control again, like whatever it was, was letting him do what he needed to do.

How could he go from so in control to drastically out of it then back again in so short a time?

He should have thought about this more deeply, considered it more, really questioned what the consequences were – but something was still blocking that side of him; the side that controlled his deeper awareness.

They approached St Helen's, the hive of chaos.

The others spoke, but he didn't hear them. Something about riot police.

"We haven't much time," Julian stated.

He looked around at the others.

Oscar. Seb. Thea.

"Do we all have what we need?" he asked.

They did.

"Then we're ready. I'm honoured to be doing this with you all. I'm not going to say may God be with us, because I have seen him on this journey. All I'll say is stay safe. We can do this. Thea, when you're ready."

The others thought this was encouragement. That this was his motivational speech.

In truth, it was his goodbye.

He came in and out of it a few more times – feeling fully aware, then not aware at all.

They began the ritual and he sat in his circle of salt, reciting the prayers. Eventually, he rose, feeling Thea's power surge through him, reciting the prayers loud and boldly so all could hear his passion.

"And those who have done good shall enter into everlasting life, but those who have done evil into everlasting fire."

He sighed.

His foot kicked out.

Had he meant to do that?

"As it was in the beginning."

The prayer was done.

He waited.

And, as he waited for Thea, he noticed something.

The circle of salt. His protection.

A gap.

One of his candles blew out.

He thought nothing of it, and awaited Thea's departure from St Helen's.

Of course, even though he was in control at this point, that was a fabrication of truth. He was granted enough control and independent thought to create the image of control; enough for him to think some of his thoughts, like a door opened to his cage but he was still tied to the bars.

After all, it was his foot kicking out that had created the gap in the circle – although he kicked his foot without intending to, and he did not consider the consequences as deeply as someone with Julian's thorough mind would.

But this gap allowed those leaving the wretched souls of St Helen's to not have to return to Hell.

It meant they all found another soul to feed on, to coerce together.

Julian celebrated, completely unaware that it was still there, and this time it had friends, all of them together, dwelling within, silently mocking him, waiting for the moment.

In fact, Julian wasn't aware of being out of control again until later that night, at 3.00 a.m., when something told him to get up, and he obeyed.

Within minutes, he was dead.

NOW

STUNNED SILENCE SURROUNDED THE SOLEMN FACES OF THE living room.

This living room had seen difficult conversations, joyous celebrations, and evenings of Oscar and April just sitting back, watching television with interlocked hands.

Now it saw Lacy setting up a bed beside an IV stand. She prepared multiple injections, using beakers to measure the dosage before sucking them into the syringe with careful precision.

Thea leant against the windowsill.

April stood by the fireplace, her elbow resting in one hand and the other hand on her face. Oscar stood next to her, wearily shifting his weight from one foot to another.

"You know," Lacy said, "this is a whole lot harder to do with you all staring at me."

Oscar looked around. He didn't want to have to tell the others to back off, he was not in the right mindset for giving orders – but it seemed that, even with a torturous death imminently looming, he would still have to take charge.

He was only just beginning to understand the burden Julian held for so long.

"She's right," he said, not sounding at all authoritative. "Let's give her some space."

Thea stood and meandered and rotated until she was staring aimlessly out of the window.

April shifted slightly so she was looking anywhere but at Lacy or Oscar.

"You know," Lacy said, "I feel it's my duty to warn you about what you are about to do."

"I know what I'm about to do." Oscar tried not to sound curt, he knew it had taken a lot for her to be here – but he could not stop thinking about what he was about to do. About what could go wrong.

About what was probably going to go wrong.

"It was many, many years ago that I did this. And with people who probably didn't share your abilities. But even when we thought it had gone right, when we thought it had all worked out – it hadn't."

She paused and looked to Oscar, who was the only one returning her stare.

"Say you do succeed. Say you do come back. You might not know if you came back alone for a long time. Years, maybe. Are you able to live with that?"

"Lacy, honestly, do you think I'd be doing this if I had a choice?"

"But you do have a choice. We could stop this right now. I could return all this equipment. I could throw these injections in the bin, pour the fluids down the toilet. It's not too late."

It was tempting.

God, it was tempting.

He'd read about Derek's attempt. Julian's intentions to make an attempt.

Was this just going to be another awful journal entry for someone else to read?

Would he even return in a fit enough state to write a journal entry – if he was to return at all?

What would he even do should he manage to arrive in Hell? Just search for the address of the devil and knock on his door?

He was going into the enemy's territory. He could be stuck there forever, enduring the worst pain known to man, for an eternity.

Hundreds of demons could swarm upon him as he arrived.

He may never even get an audience with the ruler of Hell.

Whether he did return or not, it was almost certain that his existence would not return to what it once was; that the life he had so blissfully led was over.

That he may not get to see April's smiling face again, or touch her hand, or kiss her forehead when she was upset.

But this mess was because of him.

And it was the world that would suffer if he didn't try. No one would survive, and all that he was about to lose would be lost anyway.

No, he had to do this.

He had to be stubborn about that.

He had to fight the instincts that roared at him, that desperately insisted this was a terrible decision, then go – and just hope for a miracle.

After all, they were due a miracle, weren't they?

"No," he said. "I have to do this."

"Fine," Lacy said. "I'll be ten minutes. Give me a bit of space."

Oscar looked to the others. "Shall we go to the kitchen and wait for Lacy to call us?"

Thea nodded and left.

Oscar looked to April, still with her back to him. She turned and strode past him with her head down.

"She doesn't seem to be on board," Lacy commented.

Oscar didn't answer.

"Call us when you're ready," he said, and left her to it.

42

APRIL STOOD IN THE GARDEN, LOOKING UP AT THE STARS IN THE sky. She wondered if there was another world out there, somewhere, suffering the same fate as this one.

She didn't turn around when she heard the garden door open and close. She remained still, her arms folded, her stubborn disposition intact.

She felt Oscar come close, but not close enough to touch her.

He never came that close anymore.

"You okay?" he asked.

She remembered a time when he didn't have to ask that question.

"Do you want me to leave you alone?"

She didn't answer – but, just as she felt him begin to walk away, she turned around.

"I want to go with you," she declared.

Oscar paused. Looked down. Took his time. As if he was expecting this confrontation.

"No," he said blankly, no room for manoeuvre.

"You can't tell me what I can or can't do, Oscar."

"Oh, I know," he said, smiling a little. "It's useless trying."

"So I'm going with you."

"No."

"I said you can't–"

"This is going to be difficult enough, April. I can't do this if I'm having to worry about you the whole time."

"You won't need to worry about me, I can hold my own."

"I know you can – but I will still worry. It's what I do."

She looked at him for a few seconds, thinking about the boy she'd met in the pharmacy all those years ago. When she first recruited him, he was a dork, a loser, an idiot. He had no idea what he could do and what it meant. He was set for a life working behind the checkouts, with no motivation to use the vast intelligence he so evidently had.

How different he was now.

She'd barely recognise that boy anymore.

He had become a leader. A powerful Sensitive. He was her strength.

And she desperately did not want to lose him.

"Things will change after this," she said. "It would be impossible for everything to be the same."

"Things haven't been the same for a while, April."

"You know what I mean."

He stepped toward her, finally entering her space. She could feel his breath on her, feel his presence near.

Yet, they didn't touch.

God, how she wanted to touch him.

But she couldn't bring herself to.

Just reach out, stretch your fingers, brush them down his face… That's all it would take…

But she didn't dare.

Oh, how she wished she'd dare…

"So if things are going to change, it won't matter if I come with you."

"April–"

"I can't lose you."

"I can't promise that you won't." He smiled, though she found tears in his eyes. "I can only promise that I will do my best to return this world to what it was."

"But, Oscar–"

He leant forward and seemed like he was going to kiss her, but hesitated, as if he wasn't sure it was the right thing to do. She thought about leaning in and kissing him herself, but his body retracted before she could, as if he'd just done something dirty or wrong.

"This is something I have to do. It was always going to be that way."

"But we always face these things together; we always have."

He smiled a smile one would give a child who had got a question wrong, and she felt him slip away even further.

"Not this time," he said.

Before she could reply, Thea poked her head out, announced that Lacy was ready.

He couldn't look her in the eyes.

He turned and walked back into the house.

"I love you," she said.

But he was already gone.

4 3

THE DARKER THE NIGHT BECAME, THE MORE SINISTER THE FACES were.

They went by so fast, so much bigger than him, all of them staring, as if they knew something, as if they knew that Henry was guilty.

As if they wanted to kill him for it.

He ducked his head. Tried not to look at anyone.

But he heard the whispers.

"You did it..."

He glanced over his shoulder. A couple with their arms around each other disappeared out of view.

How would they know? Why would they say that?

"You killed them..."

His head turned quickly to across the road, where he locked eyes with a woman wearing lots of makeup and ripped fishnet tights, smoking a cigarette.

"What?" she said, frowning at him. "See something you like?"

He wrapped his jacket around him for warmth. It was late

and, even though it wasn't that cold, his body shook like he was in a storm.

The faces, so pale, walking by, so many of them yet so few at all, running, walking, whispering.

He wished they would stop, but he knew they were doing nothing.

He turned a corner where the loud boom of a night club greeted him. Revellers in mirth stood outside, queueing to get in or smoking or snogging or arguing with the police.

He turned down the street.

Staying unnoticed.

He didn't realise, at first, that they had all stopped. That the bass continued to pump from the building, but their eyes were all set on him. Their expressions vacant of emotion, their eyelids ripped open, their bodies so very stationary.

A bouncer who had just been arguing with a girl over her ID now stood next to her, the ID still poised unknowingly in his hand.

The police officer wrestling a drunk, both of them, staring up at him, in the midst of a brawl on the floor.

The line of people waiting to get into the club.

The crowd outside the kebab shop.

The scantily clad woman making out with a bloke.

All of them.

Staring.

He wanted to scream, to shout *don't look at me* at the top of his voice, but it was too surreal for him to form sounds. Somehow, they all knew him.

One by one, they started to move.

One by one, they edged toward him. Those behind him, at first.

Then the queue to the club.

Then the police officers.

All of them, slowly, demented-looking, vacantly striding in his direction, pursuing him with a high-paced walk.

He sped up, looking over his shoulder again and again, only to discover they were still there.

And more were coming.

From the houses, they came. Some in pyjamas, some children, one wearing only a towel and his hair still wet.

Before he knew it, the street was full of a mass of bodies following his footsteps.

"We know what you did."

"They won't help you."

"Come with us and it will be better."

They all whispered, and he only caught the odd sentence, but each word terrified him.

He sped up his walk into a run, jogging at first. Their stride didn't break. They followed. So he sprinted.

He turned the corner and paused, hoping they weren't coming.

But he heard their footsteps, the light patter beneath the murmurs.

And more came from the houses either side of him.

A woman from a bench.

Taxi drivers from a taxi rank.

Homeless dwellers from shop windows.

So he ran, and he ran some more.

His knees wobbled, and he struggled not to fall.

He stumbled.

He cried.

He wished he wasn't alone, that someone would help him.

He didn't understand why they were doing this.

Why were they following him?

What were they?

Surely, they couldn't all be possessed?

He couldn't get a taxi, get a bus, or anything to escape. He just had to run.

Run the last few miles toward April, Oscar and Thea's home.

4 4

APRIL DIDN'T WANT TO WATCH, YET SHE COULDN'T LOOK AWAY.

Oscar sat, topless, on the edge of the bed, as Lacy fixed pads over his chest. The machine beside the bed instantly began beeping his steady heartrate – one that was far slower than her own.

Thea moved to her side. Put her arm around April's shoulders. Squeezed.

April appreciated it.

She didn't reciprocate though, and Thea soon retracted her arm, but a little gesture like this let her know she wasn't alone.

Except, she was.

Julian was gone. Oscar was going, probably for good. Thea was great, but she was young and still learning.

She was about to watch everything she had leave with Oscar's soul.

Lacy finished connecting the IV and readied three injections that she lay over a towel spread out on a side table.

"Once you are under, you will have around thirty minutes until I bring you back."

"What if I'm not done? I don't know if time will be existential where I'm going. What if–"

"Oscar, I am not going to let you die."

He sighed. Kept his face away from April.

"You have to. My body will show signs of me returning if I can, I'm sure of it."

"Okay, well then let me put it this way – you will have around half an hour until I won't be able to get you back. If you don't return in that time, your body will not be taking on enough oxygen to sustain it, and you will end up brain-dead."

Oscar closed his eyes. Nodded, as if he was really considering it – but April knew he wasn't considering it at all.

"That's fine. If I can't be brought back, then that's fine. Just wait until my body shows signs that I'm here – if it doesn't, then…"

Lacy looked to April. As if checking for her approval.

She wasn't going to get it.

"I hate having to do this," Lacy said.

"I know," said Oscar, and he placed a hand on hers. "You are not responsible for anything that goes wrong. I am doing this of my own accord. I promise."

Lacy nodded.

"Well, when you're ready then."

Oscar lay down. Stretched himself out. Closed his eyes for a moment, took in a deep breath, and let it out.

He turned to April.

Looked at her.

"Whatever happens," said Oscar, "do not give up. Keep fighting until the end. Promise?"

April didn't answer.

"Promise me," Oscar demanded.

"I promise," said April, reluctantly. "Until the end."

He turned his head and faced the ceiling. A few moments of silence passed until he eventually said those words April had been dreading:

"I'm ready."

"Okay," Lacy said, and took the first injection.

"What do they do?" April burst out.

"They will put him as close to death as he can get without actually dying. This first one puts Oscar to sleep."

She placed the first injection into the inside of Oscar's elbow, slowly pressing down on the syringe until it had emptied and Oscar's vein had received its contents.

She took the injection out and placed a tissue on the small blob of blood that appeared.

Oscar's eyes blinked quickly. He appeared groggy, then his eyes closed. April was suddenly aware that they were all staring at Oscar, all waiting for him to be completely unconscious.

A gentle snore briefly emanated from his lips.

Lacy lifted the second needle and looked to April.

April knew Lacy wasn't asking for permission, but she appreciated knowing the effects of each needle nonetheless.

"This one slows his heart rate right down," Lacy said.

She placed it into the same vein about an inch further along, pushed down, then withdrew it and dabbed the wound with the tissue.

The beep of the machine changed almost instantly. From a constant beat to a beat a second, then one every two seconds, then one every five seconds...

Eventually, the heartbeat only appeared sporadically, over intervals longer than at least thirty seconds.

"And this last one," Lacy said, readying the final needle, "well, you don't want to know what this one does."

Lacy emptied the final needle into his vein, then discarded the needle back onto the table.

She watched Oscar intently. His eyes no longer fluttered, his body no longer twitched, and his heart was barely there.

"It's done," she said. "It's up to him now."

OSCAR OPENED HIS EYES AND LIFTED HIS HEAD.

He felt empty.

White light surrounded him.

Had he been here before? All that time ago, when he was searching for answers, before he screwed the world up?

"Before you ask, you are right," came a familiar voice. "This is, as I guess you would put it, Purgatory."

He was lying down. He sat up. Turned around.

"Derek," he observed.

"Yes," Derek answered, though he didn't look pleased to see Oscar.

"I suppose you've come here to persuade me not to do this?" Oscar said, standing up and brushing himself off – although there was nothing to brush off; his trousers were immaculate.

"I am here on behalf of Heaven to do either one of two things."

"What's that?"

"Well, either I persuade you not to do this, and if I am unable to persuade you, then I am to wish you luck."

Oscar couldn't help but chuckle.

"Luck? After all the wars we've waged and fought in Heaven's name, and the best they can offer us is luck?"

"They do not meddle in human affairs like Hell does, Oscar. It was what makes them divine."

"No, it is what makes them selfish."

Derek stood. Sighed. Looked sternly at Oscar.

"I see you have grown to be quite the Sensitive. As stubborn as Julian and as foolish as I."

"I'm surprised they didn't send Julian instead of you."

"I am yet to meet Julian where I am, Oscar. Yet I live in hope. But, you see, Julian plunged himself further into Hell and hadn't the many years still living he needed to remove himself from its grip – I hope for his sake that his soul is not facing eternal damnation."

This was so unlike Derek. So forthright, so empty. He was speaking about the fate of one of his closest friends, his mentee. How could he be so callous?

Then he realised.

"You're angry with me, aren't you? For choosing April over the world."

Derek didn't reply. Instead, he just turned, said, "Come," and walked, expecting Oscar to follow – which he did.

"Heaven wishes me to relay to you that you have nothing to prove," Derek said. "That you owe the world nothing. That if it is forgiveness for your folly that you seek, then you have it."

"How could Heaven forgive me?"

Derek raised his eyebrows in an oddly accusatory fashion, and added, "Still not divine enough for you?"

He reached a pure-white bench that Oscar hadn't noticed and sat on it. Oscar did the same.

"It's your journals that led me here," Oscar said. "Yours and Julian's. Surely you meant for someone to read them. For someone to do this."

"I never expected the balance to be shifted in such a way that it would be necessary but yes, in essence, I intended to pass on my knowledge, should it be needed."

"And now? You want to stop me?"

"Heaven wants to stop you, Oscar. I am their messenger."

"And what do you want, Derek?"

Derek took a moment.

"I want a great many things. But I never found use in desiring that which is impossible to gain. I simply do what is needed."

Oscar gave up trying to decipher what Derek had said and decided to ask the important questions while he could – he didn't have that much time.

"You have two questions for me, don't you?" Derek said.

"I – yes… I do…"

"Well. Go on then."

Oscar gathered himself, then blurted out his first interrogative.

"Can I return? I mean, after this?"

Derek took a breath in through his nose, held it, and released it – which was strange, as neither of them had the need to breathe.

"Yes. I returned – though you will be needing to go far deeper into Hell than I did in order to find what you seek, and you will not have the aid of Eddie. But yes, hypothetically, you could return. That is to say, it is possible."

"I feel like there's a but."

"Well, yes, if you did by some miraculous feat or heroism manage to find safe passage back home, I would find it highly unlikely that you would return alone, or that you would ever be the same person who had left your mortal world in the first place."

Oscar nodded. In a way, it was the answer he expected.

He stood.

Realising how little time he had left, he suddenly felt hasty.

"Don't worry," said Derek. "Time doesn't exist in this world as it does in yours. It's not going anywhere."

"Fine. My second question…"

"Yes? Go on, ask it."

"Can I actually be successful? As in, can I confront the devil, God's equivalent? Can I beat him? Can I actually end this?"

Derek stood also.

"Ah. Well there is the conundrum that can't be solved."

"Why not?"

"Because, my dear boy, no ordinary human has ever made it that far into Hell and returned to tell us what happened. There is no way of knowing. You are entering, as they say, the realm of the unknown. A witness has never contested that you can, or that you can't."

"And Heaven? What if I don't do this, what then? Do I return to my world? Do I die?"

"They would be willing to grant you safe passage into Heaven. You would live the rest of eternity in happiness, knowing you were safe."

"And the rest of the world?"

Derek didn't answer.

"And April?"

He simply tilted his head and gave the slightest shrug of his shoulders.

"What would you do?" Oscar asked.

"Ah, another question. I would consider it to be incredibly stupid, and incredibly risky."

Oscar dropped his head.

Derek placed a firm hand on Oscar's shoulder.

"But, like you, I would keep trying until the very end."

Oscar lifted his head. Looked to Derek.

It was sad, how much he would have benefitted from

Derek's tutorage. His guidance was exactly what he needed and, should Derek have still been with them, Oscar was sure the fight wouldn't have ended up this way.

"Then down I go," said Oscar.

"Down you go," echoed Derek.

And, in a vast whoosh, Derek disappeared, the white light shot upwards, and he found himself plummeting downwards at speeds he could not quite comprehend.

THEA WATCHED OSCAR'S HELPLESS BODY EMPTY. IT WAS strange, how he looked asleep, yet vacant – like there was something that had left, something that was no longer there.

She hesitated to look at April, but she did. April was frantically switching between staring at Oscar, turning away and closing her eyes, and looking out of the window.

Lacy stuck rigidly by Oscar's side, a finger on his pulse despite the machine telling her all she needed to know.

And that's when she felt it.

In her gut, rising up through her lungs, choking her, alarm ringing through her mind, her arms shaking.

Something was wrong.

"What is it?" April asked. Thea hadn't been aware April was looking at her.

"I don't know…" Thea answered honestly.

She left the living room for the hallway, where she stood, just watching, waiting, listening.

Something was here.

"What?" April said, appearing behind her, her rising anxiety in contrast to Thea's cool collectedness.

Thea didn't answer.

She closed her eyes.

Stayed as still as she could keep herself.

A soft nudge pushed gently against her shoulder.

She opened her eyes and turned to April. She looked terrified.

"Was that you?" Thea asked.

"Was what me?"

Footsteps beat against the floor upstairs, so quiet Thea thought she may have been mistaken if April hadn't twitched in response too.

"Is there someone in the house?" April called, stepping forward. Thea placed an arm across her.

"Don't," Thea instructed.

She listened.

Absolute silence was met with a sickening wail, like a screaming banshee, forcing them to their knees. They covered their ears. It was over as quick as it came, but the reverberation continued to shake every loose item for a good few seconds after.

"What's going on?" Lacy called from in the living room.

Before Thea could respond, she was taken from her feet and thrown into the kitchen.

Every drawer opened and closed, the crockery on the drying board vibrated, and the chairs rattled across the floor.

"Thea?" April snapped. "What is it?"

"Oscar said this could happen," Thea said, though she was trying to convince herself as much as April. This felt like something else.

A few heavy knocks announced themselves upon the front door.

April gasped and turned to Thea.

"Don't answer it," April said.

"That isn't it," Thea said, feeling that the knock on the door hadn't come from something otherworldly, but from something in need. "That's something else."

She pushed herself to her feet and, ignoring an invisible barge that knocked her to the side, she made it to the door and swung it open.

There stood the boy. Henry. His quivering body a wreck, tears bombarding his cheeks.

"Help me!" he cried.

Thea grabbed him and pulled him inside.

"What are you doing?" Thea demanded. "You were told to go home!"

"There's something after me!" Henry said. "There's lots of them, and they are following me, and I can't get away!"

Thea looked out of the door, trying to see whatever it was that had made Henry so perturbed. She saw nothing.

But she felt everything.

She slammed the door shut.

For a moment, whatever had been attacking them ceased. Stopped. Finished.

"Is it gone?" April asked.

It had stopped, but it hadn't gone.

It was simply the eye of the storm.

"I can feel something here," April said. "It's trying to speak through me."

"Don't let it," Thea said, suddenly aware that she was giving an older and far more experienced Sensitive instructions.

She looked to Henry and his distraught, crying face.

To April, looking to her for guidance, too messed up to act, unable to pick up on all that Thea was picking up on.

To Oscar, Lacy by his side.

This could all go so very wrong if they didn't act quickly.

"Thea," April said. "Please, tell us what you're picking up on that I'm not. Tell us what it is."

Thea did not know what it was. She had the gift, but none of the knowledge.

But she knew, without a doubt, that something was there, and that Henry had just brought it with him.

"Barricade the house," she said. "We're under attack."

Oscar's back thudded against rock and he felt every bone and every muscle scream upon impact as if his senses had been multiplied by ten.

He lay there, groaning, willing the pain to subside. There was a smell of burning. Black smoke hovered overhead. Thrashing, like waves against waves except louder and with more intensity, did little to mute the mass of screams that came at him in an onslaught of surround-sound agony.

He leant up, rubbing the back of his skull, feeling a migraine throb from the back to the front of his head.

He looked around. He hadn't known what to expect, but this was something else – he was on a single rock, no bigger than his kitchen table, lava spewing and snapping at him with such aggression it was as if it was being conducted by a raging bull.

Even worse than the pain and the horizon of fire was that feeling – like despair, only more hopeless. Like everything was awful and it could never get better and this was just the beginning of the suffering.

He tried to get to his feet, but as soon as he moved, pain shot up his spine and stretched his body with a scream.

Mad cackling reverberated over the distant screams of anguish, shrieks belonging to souls he couldn't see.

Being here for a minute was unbearable. The sudden fear that, should he fail to return, he would spend an eternity here, caused him mental torture to match his pain. He hadn't even met anything yet, seen anything, confronted anything. Nothing had started his torture, his eternity of suffering, and already it was unbearable.

The lava flicked itself further and a lash of it splashed over his foot. He recoiled, wincing until he could wince no further and the throbbing forced a screech. The stroke of lava turned his foot black, the smell like burnt bacon, a tinge of smoke rising from his bare skin.

It was only now that he looked down and saw that he was wearing the clothes he was wearing before, only now they were rags, a few ripped pieces of cloth barely covering his dignity. His feet were bare, and the soles were burning under the heat of the rock.

He dropped to his knees, feeling the spikes of stone cut his knees and leave bloody patches on the mound beneath him.

He had to deal with it.

He had to cope.

He had to somehow find a way to bury the pain and do what he had come here to do.

But it didn't stop, didn't let up, no break to the constant spurts of lava or the buzzing ache shooting up and down his body.

He let out a large, defiant scream in order to resist a scream of pain.

"Come out!" he shouted, though he wasn't sure who at.

Cackling sung beneath the symphony of screams, growing

into a crescendo, like an orchestra playing tunes of misery, a hundred discordant notes colliding in a cacophony of awful sounds.

"Come on, you bastard. I know you're there!"

A shadow swung above, only visible out of the corner of his eye.

He reached for the crucifix in his pocket, but his pocket wasn't even there. He had no defence, nothing to battle these things with.

How had he ever thought this was possible?

How had he considered that, for a moment, he even stood a chance? He was unarmed, uneducated, and unable to face what was inevitably coming.

"Come on!" he growled with as much force as his throat could allow. It felt like he'd swallowed razor blades and they were trying to burst out from his skin.

A few more shadows soared past, laughing and chuckling and screeching with joy.

"You don't scare me!" he lied.

They swung lower, and he could make out a silhouette of horns on one, and the dark imitation of three snapping heads on another.

He had faced these demons as they possessed the bodies of people – so what if he now saw them as they were?

It meant nothing.

I can face them.

As confidently as he thought this, he struggled to believe it.

"Stop taunting me and show yourselves!"

The shadows came lower, spinning and spinning until Oscar found himself being circled, preyed upon, entwined in a constant spiral of silhouettes.

He looked straight ahead to avoid himself becoming dizzy.

It didn't work.

"You don't scare me," he insisted.

The laughing intensified.

"Laugh all you want! I know what you are!"

The spinning grew and grew and grew in speed, more vigorous and intently and belligerently and antagonistically and he fell to his knees unable to take it their voices screaming inside his head screaming and screaming and *oh my God they are inside me inside my head get out get out get out get out I–*

He covered his ears, but they were already there. Digging their fingers in, forcing him to his bloody knees. It felt like his brain was expanding, growing bigger and bigger, pressing against his skull, bursting against it trying to make it bigger but it wouldn't get bigger it wouldn't *please get out my head get out my head I can't take it I can't–*

They stopped circling.

A momentary respite allowed him to lift his head.

There they were. A mass of them, all different sights, some with horns, some with tails, with heads of animals, legs of animals, tails of serpents – every kind of demon there was, set out before him.

"Is this how you greet everyone?" Oscar asked. "This many of you in the welcoming ceremony?"

"*No!*" one said.

"*Only for a Sensitive!*" said another.

"*Only for a servant of Heaven!*" said another.

He couldn't place the voices, couldn't tell who was saying what, but they went on, on and on and on.

"*You made a mistake coming here, Oscar Ecstavio...*"

As correct as such an assertion was, he couldn't give up now.

He had to work harder, even though their torture had only begun.

"I demand an audience with your ruler," Oscar demanded. "I demand an audience with the devil."

His demand was met with more raucous laughter, the kind that only served to mock and demean him.

That laughter let him know, in no uncertain terms, that he was irreparably, unequivocally stuck.

All he could think of was April, her face smiling back at him, and how he'd never get to see her again.

April was grateful for Thea taking charge.

For being so brave. So different from the scared little girl who had arrived here not so long ago.

It wasn't that April couldn't lead, or that she thought herself inferior. Nor was it because of Thea's greater abilities that gave her the authority.

It was because she could think of nothing but Oscar.

She was not thinking of the oncoming attack, however that may manifest. She was not thinking of defences, of ways to fight, of how to keep the evil spirits out.

She was thinking of how to protect his body whilst he did what he had to.

She rushed back into the living room, leaving the other two to do what they needed.

"What's going on?" Lacy asked.

April glanced at the clock. He had been under for ten minutes. They just had to keep him safe for another twenty.

Assuming he makes it back in that twenty.

"Something's coming," April answered.

"What? What's coming?"

"We don't know. But it's bad."

A screech from the hallway attracted her attention.

April looked at Oscar, hovering, wanting to help Thea but not wanting to leave him.

"It's fine," Lacy assured her. "He's safe. Go help them."

She arrived in the hallway to find Henry pinned against the wall by nothing, then left to drop and land painfully on his arm.

Thea, who had been beginning to fix a piece of wood against the front door, rushed to Henry.

"It's no good barricading the doors," April said. "It's already in here."

Thea went to reply, only to find herself pushed back against the wall.

"No!" she shouted, and she freed herself from whatever had her.

Shuffles of footsteps could be heard. They ran to the nearest window and looked out.

Faces appeared in the distance. A mass of them. Walking closer.

"That's them..." Henry said, wiping sweat from his eyes.

Thea and April looked at each other, both lost, both clueless. They could not barricade the doors in time – nor could they stop what was already inside from getting to them.

"We're not going to be able to stop them getting in," Thea admitted, looking to April despairingly, out of ideas.

"Fine," April said. "But we must keep them out of the living room. We must keep them away from Oscar."

Thea nodded. It was the best idea they had.

They went to walk back into the living room, but the door slammed shut before they could.

April pulled and pulled on the door handle, but it did not budge.

"Move aside," Thea said, and April did so.

Thea took her crucifix pendant from around her neck, lifted it out, held it, focussed, then bellowed, *"Move!"*

The door instantly flung open.

She grabbed Henry and ran inside the living room, April following and slamming the door behind her.

Without saying anything, April and Thea moved the sofa in front of the door.

"This isn't going to be enough," Thea said.

"We can't keep them out by barricading us in," April agreed. "But there is something that can keep them out."

"What?"

April looked at her expectantly.

"No!" Thea said, shaking her head and waving her arms. "No, no, no, no. I can't fight evil spirits and a whole army of... No, April, I can't."

April placed a hand on her shoulder.

"This is why you are here, Thea," April said. "This is the reason you came. Why we found you. This is the great thing you are able to do that will help save us."

Thea shook her head.

"Please," April said. "At least try."

She held Thea's gaze, held it with all she had, trying to tell her everything she needed to with a look.

Thea nodded ever so slightly.

"Do it," April said, and ran back to Oscar's side.

Thea turned to Henry. She took her crucifix from her pocket and presented it to him.

"I'm going to need some help," Thea said.

Henry looked at the crucifix like she was handing him a corpse's head.

"I – I – I can't..." he stuttered.

"No. But you can at least try."

He took the crucifix. She didn't wait for him to rise; she

pulled him to his feet herself and they stood, facing the door, ready for war.

April interlocked her fingers with Oscar's, kissing his hands softly, and gazed at his absent face.

"Come on, Oscar," she whispered. "You can do this."

Oscar rose to his feet, ignoring the searing pain of his calves, rejecting the throbbing of his cranium, refuting the fiery shots of agony up and down his veins – he was not giving in.

"Laugh all you want," he snarled, "I am not leaving until I have had an audience with him."

More cackles, all of different pitches, some screeching, some piercing, some low, all vile.

"You're right..."

"He's right..."

"You are never leaving..."

He spread his arms out in an attempt to make a crucifix with his body, holding this position rigidly, in place, determined not to be broken.

"I demand it!" he bellowed. "The Lord demands it – no, the Lord compels you!"

"Your God has no dominion here..."

"I demand it as I stand in the shape of the cross, that which Jesus–"

A slash of what felt like a hot whip spread across his back and he fell once more to his knees.

He rose, once again standing tall, standing strong.

"Does the crucifix offend you?"

"The crucifix..."

"Is a representation..."

"Of when evil prevailed..."

"It invigorates us..."

"Powers us..."

"AROUSES US..."

"Do you think you can intimidate me?"

Another lash and he fell to his knees, his palms hurting from the pressure of his nails, but he stood once again, against his better judgement, against the unrelenting pain of his body.

"I cannot be broken. I command—"

Another lash.

Then another.

And another.

And another.

He paused, huddled on his knees, coughing blood; he did not know whether this blood even existed, but it lurched up through his throat, nonetheless.

But that was it – in Purgatory, his soul had been existential. In Hell, he felt his body, remaining mortal but refusing to die.

Suffering without the release of death seemed like the best torture they could give him.

But losing the world, losing against all that he'd fought against, losing April – these were things worse than pain upon his mortal body.

He rose once again, his back burning, something trickling down the back of his legs, probably blood, possibly puss.

He wiped sweat from his forehead.

"He does not submit..."

"He thinks he's fighting for something..."

"He does not learn..."

"I *am* fighting for something," asserted Oscar defiantly. "And what are you fighting for? Dominion over a world you can't claim? The pleasure of inflicting pain? All you are, are rejects of Heaven."

Another lash. He growled, but refused to bow to his knees this time.

"That's what you are, isn't it? Fallen angels?"

Another lash. He screamed, then kept the scream going once the immediate pain had subsided, turning the scream from anguish to insolence, from pain to resolve.

"You were in Heaven, you disobeyed their laws, so they sent you down here to be the shit of the immortal world."

Another.

"Heaven didn't want you."

Another.

"And maybe that's why you are so fucking bitter."

Another, and this time he did collapse to his knees, feeling his entire body groan. His fingers gripped loose stones, his body tensed, but the pain was too great, and it would not go away.

"One more time," he said, then spat out a mouthful of blood and what was possibly a tooth. "I command you, unclean spirits, evil dwellers, bitches of God – take. Me. To. Him."

Another lash. He stayed on his knees. Another, another, another – then they stopped, very suddenly.

Something appeared behind him. He heard hooves thumping the floor.

The demons hovering before him all looked to this thing like it was in charge, like it was something stronger than them, like they were in trouble.

He looked up. He could see the outline of three heads, though his vision was struggling to focus. One a ram, one a bull, one a man. Flaming eyes. Tail of a serpent.

Oscar recognised the traits from his studies.

This was Balam. One of the devil's princes, commanding many legions of Hell.

"The devil has heard you," said Balam, his voice booming through the distance. "He will grant your audience."

Oscar closed his eyes, relieved, as if the torture was over.

Then he reminded himself not to be so naïve.

If the devil had granted him an audience, it would be for his own purpose. This was far from over.

In fact, it was probably only just beginning.

"Take me to him," Oscar said, wiping blood from his back.

50

THEA AND HENRY STOOD DEFIANTLY, THEIR CRUCIFIXES READY, clutched securely in their hands, glaring at the door.

April did not. She knelt next to Oscar's bed, glancing at the clock, to him, to the clock, to him.

He had five minutes until his thirty were up.

She did not look at Lacy.

She *could not* look at Lacy.

She did not want to hear that they were running out of time, that it would soon be too late, that she would have lost Oscar forever.

The sounds began. Stubborn footsteps. Barging against the front door. The garden door smashing and the kitchen being opened up.

A gust of wind battered against the living room door and Thea and Henry pushed the sofa back up against it.

"Henry," Thea said, with a poor attempt to disguise the wobble in her voice. "Repeat after me. Father, I consecrate this home to you."

"Father, I consecrate this home to you," came Henry's voice, tiny and hidden away, as if in a box somewhere.

"Louder!" Thea demanded. "Father, I consecrate this home to you!"

"Father, I consecrate this home to you!" His voice was louder, but its shake was obvious.

More and more footsteps could be heard approaching the house. Wind battered against the shaking door.

Thea raised her cross.

Henry copied.

"I declare this property under His kingdom and His jurisdiction, and you are forbidden from manifesting here!"

Henry repeated her words exactly, every word a struggle, every syllable full of terror.

April squeezed Oscar's hand tighter, wishing it would squeeze back, praying she would feel him return.

The clock kept ticking next to her. Another minute passed, and her hope was diminishing with every second.

"When I speak, you shout hear my prayer," Thea instructed Henry. "In His name I break all rituals, curses or hexes that may keep you here!"

"Hear my prayer!"

"Louder, Henry! Mean it!"

"Hear my prayer!"

"Come on, Oscar," April whispered, loud enough so only she could hear. "Please come back to me. Please, please..."

"I stand in His authority and my own, commanding you to go!"

"Hear my prayer!"

"I'm sorry, Oscar, I'm so, so sorry... I should never have pushed you away. If you come back to me, I promise, I promise..."

"April–" Lacy said.

"No!" she screamed. "No!"

She did not want to hear how long was left. She did not want to hear that they were close to losing him, she did not want it confirmed, verbally or otherwise, that she would not get him back.

"April, he's–"

"No! Stop it!"

April buried her head in Oscar's chest, feeling his t-shirt soak with tears, not caring, just wanting him back, just desperately praying for him to return.

"Please, Oscar, come back. Lord, please bring him back, please…"

The Lord had never answered her prayer before, but now was a time to start.

The door was beating against its hinges so furiously that the wall beside it was starting to crack. Bangs against the walls from the beating fists of invaders caused pictures of Oscar and April to rattle off the walls and land on the floor.

"Oscar… Come on…"

"I bow with my heart and ask You for protection from the evil ones," Thea persisted, grit and tenacity strengthening her. "Surround us with a shield and keep us in it."

"Hear my prayer!"

Even Henry's voice grew stronger, for all the good it was doing.

Still, the attackers remained outside the door.

Thea was giving them time.

Something they had so little of.

"April–" Lacy tried again.

"No!"

"April, you can't keep saying this. He has a minute left, and then…"

She shook.

This couldn't be happening.

This couldn't.

There was no way.

She wasn't going to let it.

She looked up at Lacy, aware of what a mess she looked, how distraught she was.

"Send me in," she said, softly and quiet.

"What?"

"Send me in," she repeated, this time louder, this time realising what she was saying.

"No," Lacy said, frantically shaking her head. "No, no, no – my agreement was with Oscar, to send him in. I'm not sending you in as well–"

"I'm not asking you!" April shouted. "I'm going in after him, with your help or without it!"

"April, you will die too."

She paused.

Let those words settle.

Then began to ready herself.

"Prepare the needles," she instructed.

OVER MASSES OF STONES AND LAVA AND CLIFFS HE SOARED, HELD loosely by the claws of Balam. Below, he could see wretched souls in their suffering, demons tearing them apart and feasting on their insides, impaling them, castrating them, ripping their jaws open, then putting them back together so the demon could just do it all over again.

He wanted to save them, but he knew it wasn't why he was here. Besides, even if he wanted to, there was nothing he could do.

This was not his dominion.

He had to remember that.

Eventually, Balam landed, his hooves pounding the ground, throwing Oscar carelessly to the cracked and bumpy stone surface.

The sky was scorched, full of sickening, dark amber mixed with black smoke, giving nothing but an omen of blackness over the large rock he found himself on.

He pushed himself to his knees.

"Well?" Oscar said. "Where is he?"

"I am not here to make the introduction," Balam said. "I now have to go await the other one."

"The other one?" Oscar repeated. "What other one?"

Balam grinned, then flew off, leaving Oscar to his solitary panic.

The other one?

There was no other one... Did Balam mean a person? Another demon, maybe? Was Derek coming down to help?

No, that didn't feel right.

What other one?

It didn't matter. It was a trick, something to create confusion.

He had to focus.

This was his chance.

"Well?" he shouted, hearing his question bounce back at him multiple times. "Where are you?"

A low hum of laughter hung on the air.

"That doesn't scare me," Oscar said. "Laugh all you want."

The rock shook, like something had just landed on it, and he looked around, rotating repeatedly to try and see what was there.

A fog approached, and within that fog, a figure.

"Is that you?"

The figure walked forward, as if the fog was accompanying it. Its feet moved with a light tapping. The figure was the same size as Oscar, and there was little demonic about it. This wasn't what he was expecting.

Was this a trick?

How foolish he was to think they would actually show him the devil.

From the fog, the figure emerged.

In a suit. A dark, sinister orange face with horns and a tail, but with the body of a man, and wearing a suit.

A damn suit.

Oscar shook himself out of it.

Why would…

No. It was all part of the trick. All part of the way demons try and mess with your head.

He was appearing like this to taunt him.

He had to focus.

Not let it get to him.

It approached, coming closer, until it stood within inches of Oscar.

They looked at one another, saying nothing. Its face looked smug, condescending, and Oscar was unsure why he was not feeling complete agony.

The devil brought a hand out of his pocket, opening a small metal case, and presenting a few cigarettes.

"Care for one?" he asked.

Oscar stared at the cigarettes, then to the devil.

"No," Oscar said.

"Probably for the best. Those things will kill you."

He discarded the box.

He grinned.

"Look at you," the devil said. "You don't know what to say, do you?"

Oscar looked over his shoulder, looked around himself, as if waiting for the real ruler of Hell to appear.

"It's me," he said. "Don't worry, you're not confused."

Oscar stuttered over words, trying to find the right things to say.

"After all this time, you were expecting something different, weren't you?"

"Y – yes…"

"Then don't piss me off."

"Huh?"

"I said, then don't piss me off."

The devil meandered a few steps away, his back to Oscar, and looked out over the horizon, closing his eyes and soaking up the distant screams.

"So," he said. "You've come here to plead with me to stop my assault on your world. Is that correct?"

"Er...yes."

"Okay then." He turned back to Oscar. "Plead with me."

Oscar didn't know what to say.

"This isn't a trick," the devil assured him. "We have a bit of time before she gets here. Plead with me."

"Before who gets here? Who is coming?"

"Like I said, we need to kill a bit of time while we wait. So plead with me."

"I'm not going to grovel."

"Well that's fairly poor pleading, then."

"Just... stop. Stop what you're doing."

The devil paused. Raised an eyebrow.

"That it?" he said. "Huh. Not the worst I've seen, I guess..."

The devil sighed and looked around, as if growing bored by Oscar's inept argument.

"It's not your world," Oscar said. "This is your world. Leave it alone."

The devil shrugged.

"You don't need it."

"Need? Oh, Oscar, this was never about need. It is about want."

"But–"

"I have wanted your world for many, many eternities. I have been biding my time since before your species evolved. I have been waiting and waiting and waiting for the moment, and you gave it to me, you created an imbalance that allowed it – and now you think that your demand will work? You think you coming here and telling me to leave it alone like some little prissy fool is going to make me relinquish control over a world I am so very close to taking?"

"Close? But you're not close."

"Alas, you are accurate with that – I have just one more thing to do. And that is why I wait for her to arrive."

"Who is *her?*"

The devil chuckled.

"Listen, you sack of shit," he said, charging forward. "I will fight you and I will–"

"You will fight me?" the devil echoed. "Okay, go on then. Let's see this."

Oscar did nothing. He thought about throwing a punch, but knew how little that would do. It all felt so wrong. So make-believe. So unreal.

"You're pathetic," Oscar said.

"Oh yes?" the devil said with a chuckle.

"You get cast out of Heaven, create your own cult of rejects, then think you can just take what's not yours?"

"Why yes, I imagine that would be fairly accurate."

"Well, I'm better than you."

The devil grimaced slightly, a small change to his smug pleasure.

"The Sensitives are all better than you."

His grimace grew, and his rage grew, and Oscar could feel it reaching out to him like fire licking his face.

"Derek, Julian, me. Eddie King. All of us. We are better than you."

"I said not to piss me off."

"And we will beat you."

"I warned you."

"And we will laugh at you. While. You. Beg."

The devil roared, and the imitation of a human body instantly morphed, the suit turning to flames, his body growing bigger, bigger, a body of fire, horns that were twice the size of Oscar. Its claws curled and sharpened, its tail whipping and slashing, its eyes reddening, until it had grown into a large, powerful beast full of rage and menace.

Now this felt right.

Now this looked like the real devil.

THE WALLS WERE SHAKING, THE HOUSE WAS SHAKING, AND THEY were shaking. Thea and Henry continued their prayers, continued battling as best they could – but their resistance was breaking.

The floor began to tremble.

The walls began to quiver.

Their resolve began to fade.

April ignored all of it.

She lay on the sofa, staring at the shaking ceiling, holding an arm out for Lacy.

"Are you sure about–"

"Do it!" April commanded.

Lacy finished preparing the first injection and pushed it into her arm.

She felt herself drift into sleep.

She felt the next prick but wasn't aware of it.

She sank away, falling deeper and deeper and deeper until–

A white room greeted her. Nothing but bright light.

She didn't know where she was, but she knew well enough that she wasn't where she intended to be.

"What is this?" she asked, with no one to answer.

She ran back and forth, looking around. There must be some way...

"You absolute fool," came the wise voice of Derek.

She turned and looked at him.

A sudden rush of questions came to her in a moment and left just as quickly. She had one thing she wanted to know, and she would not leave without knowing it.

"How do I get to Hell?" she asked.

"April, you are not meant to be here," Derek said.

"I don't care! How do I get there?"

"April, please–"

"Do not waste my time!" she shouted, her voice echoing.

"You were not supposed to do this," Derek insisted. "This was Oscar's task, and Oscar's alone."

"And you think I'm going to sit by and let Oscar die?"

"You think you can do anything to stop him dying? You think doing this is aiding him in any way?"

"Derek, would you just–"

"Don't you see? This is playing into his hands. This is exactly what the devil wanted!"

April considered this for a moment, then discarded the information. She resisted tears, albeit unsuccessfully. She urged Derek with her melancholy look, did all she could to beseech him, to beg of him.

"Derek, please. I can't be here. I have to–"

"You are making the same mistake Oscar made all those months ago," Derek said. "When will you two grow up and realise – this whole thing is bigger than you."

"I love him–"

"Many people have loved many people over the course of history, April. And many people have had to let them go."

April marched up to him, unsure what she planned to do

once she arrived. She stood her ground, wanting to do something drastic, but knowing she needed his help.

"This is not what is meant to happen," Derek continued. "If you do this, then… You have no idea what could happen. What *will* happen."

"You were in love once. Right? I know it was a long time ago, but you were."

He didn't answer.

"What would you have done?"

Derek stroked his beard and considered her.

"No one said this was easy, April."

"Oh, leave the clichés." She turned and walked in circles, looking around, and began shouting, "Send me to Hell! Send me to Hell! I want to get to Hell!"

"April–"

"I know you can hear me! Send me there, now!"

"April, please–"

"Send me there!"

She turned to look at Derek, her lip curling, fists clenching, her foot tapping.

"It's below us, isn't it?" she asked.

Derek's eyes widened.

That was her confirmation.

She threw her fist downwards at the floor.

"April, please don't do this."

She threw her fist downwards once again and the bright white light began to crack.

"April, you are going to fundamentally end the world because of your stupidity!"

She threw her whole body downwards, feeling herself getting closer.

"April, this is not what's meant to happen!"

She looked up at him one last time.

"Goodbye, Derek," she said.

With a final punch the floor disappeared, and she found herself plummeting into the depths of Hell.

53

THEA LOOKED OVER HER SHOULDER AT APRIL'S BODY, LYING ON the sofa, devoid of life.

"This is going to make them stronger," Thea told Henry. "With Oscar and April both gone, the balance is shifted even further."

"What do we do?" he asked.

Thea looked to Lacy, who averted her terrified stare from one body to the other.

"We need to leave the room, so they follow us," Thea said.

"What?" Henry exclaimed.

Thea knew how he felt. The last thing she wanted was to go out among them.

But she had to think about the mission.

She had to draw them away from Oscar and April and do everything she could to give them a fighting chance.

"Lacy," Thea said, and Lacy's head suddenly snapped out of whatever trance she was in. "We are going out. Barricade this door once we're gone."

"Are you kidding? You can't leave me alone in here!"

"We are going to drag them away, it's the only chance we have."

The door battered from side to side. Its crack grew bigger. And bigger. It was about to break.

Thea looked around, looking for a way out.

"We're going to have to go through the window," she said and, before Henry could object, she opened it and leapt through.

Many, many pale, demented faces turned to look at her.

She thought there had been ten, maybe twenty.

Not this many.

She stared at them, and they stared back.

Then they advanced.

Henry climbed out of the window and Lacy shut it behind him. Thea glanced back at Lacy's petrified frown, watched her back into the shadows of the room.

The crowd seemed to follow her.

As did the wind. Everywhere she went, it shook the branches, pushed leaves into the air, wobbled the fence.

"We have to keep the prayers going, Henry," she urged him. She raised her crucifix and he did the same.

"I ask that You protect our minds."

"Hear my prayer!"

"Father, the mind set on the flesh is death, but the mind set on the Spirit is peace."

"Hear my prayer!"

"By your power, protect us."

"Hear my prayer!"

They kept coming.

Kept advancing.

The prayers doing little to deter them.

So she stopped backing away.

Stopped running.

"What are you doing?" cried Henry.

"The prayers aren't working," she said.

"Then we need to run!"

"No, Henry. The prayers aren't working because we're afraid. Because we don't mean it."

"What!"

She turned toward him, seeing a face much like her own from only a short time ago, when she was wrung with fear.

She took his hand.

"We do this together," she said.

He didn't reply.

"We do it, ready for what happens, completely unafraid. Do you trust me?"

He nodded.

That was all she needed.

Together, they strode forward, holding out their crucifixes.

"Whatever is true, whatever is pure, whatever is honourable is worthy of You – let our minds dwell only on these things."

"Hear my prayer!"

They emerged themselves amongst the bodies until they were surrounded, submerged; both of them obstinately, unwaveringly, unquestionably fearless.

OSCAR COWERED.

There was nothing else he could do.

The poor imitation of a man had gone and this great, fiery beast had taken its place. Bigger and grander than any demon he knew of, bursting with fire.

Oscar tried to say, *I am not afraid.*

But he couldn't.

He could barely form the first syllable.

"Beg now, Sensitive!" it mocked, its voice wickedly majestic. "Beg for mercy for your world!"

Oscar backed away, crawling backwards, but he couldn't even see the end of its shadow.

He could say nothing, do nothing, and feel everything. Every sin he'd committed came rushing back to him, every act of nastiness flooding his mind, forcing him to relive every moment that meant he deserved a place in Hell.

The devil was doing this.

He knew that.

And he had to stop it. Had to resist.

But there was no resisting. There was no barrier he could put up against strength like this.

"Stop it!" he screamed, but his plea only met laughter.

Every bad word he'd called somebody, every argument where he was wrong, and every time he sulked for not getting what he wanted.

Projected like a cinema screen he couldn't look away from.

The laughter of kids as they teased him, as they taunted him, as they bullied him until he was too angry to not snap back.

Then it all stopped.

All of it, ceasing abruptly.

He collapsed, panting, exhausted.

He allowed his mind to re-find sense, to rediscover his own thoughts, to register his own senses.

But why had it stopped?

He looked up, awaiting an explanation – but the devil was not looking at him.

The devil was still grinning, but at something over his shoulder.

Balam set its hooves down against the rock, prompting a minor quake.

From his back he took something and threw it down.

A woman.

Balam left, and the woman rolled onto her back.

Oscar knew that woman.

And, as she gained her feet, he felt everything good in his life crumble, everything he was fighting for diminish, and he was beaten, defeated.

April pushed herself to her feet.

"What are you doing here?" Oscar screamed.

April ran forward, rushing toward an embrace, only to find that she couldn't reach him. Something stopped her. Something in between them, keeping them apart.

The devil's mocking laughter made it clear who had put up this invisible barrier.

"April, I told you–"

"Oscar, you've been here for too long. You need to come back. You're going to go brain-dead."

"That was always a possibility, April, you knew that. This is – what are you doing?"

"See, Oscar," spoke the devil, and Oscar twisted to peer at him over his shoulder. "I told you we just needed to wait for her to arrive."

Henry looked to Thea in awe. The way she held herself, the power she had, the way she did so much despite being so young. He'd heard that she'd only been discovered by the Sensitives weeks before he arrived – yet she commanded these demons with such ferociousness it was almost intimidating.

"God, by Your name, save me, and by Your might defend my cause!" she barked.

The faces swarmed around them, yet when she said her prayer with such passion and such belief, her hand seemed to command them to back away.

"Henry, the answer!"

The answer?

Oh, yes!

"Hear my prayer!" he shouted, his voice tiny and childish compared to hers.

"For haughty men have risen up against me and fierce men seek my life!"

"Hear my prayer!"

All of those faces, those vessels, those empty bodies that

had followed, terrified him, shaken him – they seemed pathetic now. Like vacant minds with nowhere to go.

Another line of them fell to their knees, clutching their chests, looking up to the sky. Henry could swear he saw something rise up out of one of them, a shrieking entity dispersing between their lips.

"Turn back the evil upon my foes, in Your faithfulness, destroy them!"

"Hear my prayer!"

A wave of them collapsed, arms raised, screaming, then fell to their backs, not so pale anymore, not so empty, looking scared and confused.

"Your turn, Henry!" Thea shouted above the cries of terror and relief.

"What?"

"Remember the prayer you practised."

At first, Henry was confused. He couldn't remember reciting any incantations.

Then he recalled.

It felt like years ago, but was only days. He had stood before the mirror, made to say these words with passion, and froze up when put on the spot.

He had been scared back then, without knowing what true fear was.

He had lost friends.

He had lost his purpose.

He had lost everything for the other recruits who wished to fight.

Now was the time to stop focussing on everything that went wrong – and start to believe in what would go right.

"Holy Mother of God," he went to say.

"Louder!" Thea commanded. "Mean it!"

Mean it.

The words spun around his disorganised mind.

I have to mean it.

He held the cross outwards, strengthening his arm, clutching, flexing his fingers, his lip curling into a defiant snarl.

"Holy Mother of God," he bellowed, his voice as he had never heard his voice before. "Holy Virgin of virgins!"

"Good," Thea told him.

He looked one pale-faced man in the eyes, no longer terrified by its blank visage.

"Depart, transgressor!" he shouted.

"Together!" Thea said, and she too raised her cross, and she too directed it at the same wretched soul.

"Depart, transgressor!" they both commanded. *"Depart, seducer, full of lies and cunning."*

The man fell, wriggling, seizing, until he was on his back and his mouth was open and he was staring with wide eyes as something slid out of him and he looked around in confusion.

He'd done it.

I did it, I did it, I actually did it!

Astonished at his own ability, he continued to point the crucifix at more of them, as Thea continued to do the same.

Together, they repeated.

"Depart transgressor. Depart, seducer, full of lies and cunning."

More fell.

More collapsed.

More seized.

They weren't just ceasing their attacking – they were being freed. No longer slaves to whatever entity was controlling them, no longer suffering inside of their own bodies.

"Depart, transgressor!"

He felt the power surge through him.

"Depart, seducer, full of lies!"

He felt the power of being a Sensitive.

261

"No..." SOBBED OSCAR. "No..."

He placed himself between April and the lord of the underworld, as if that would do something, as if he couldn't just brush him aside.

"What do you plan to do?" he asked, so feebly he had to repeat himself with more conviction. "What do you plan to do?"

The devil approached, and Oscar backed off, keeping himself in front of April.

"You will not take her," Oscar said defiantly.

"I will take what I want," the devil retorted, His grin never fading. "Do you not know who I am?"

"I know who you are. And you will not have her!"

The Devil didn't even need to flinch or raise his hand for Oscar to find himself flailing through the scorched air and onto his back, twenty-odd yards away.

He tried not to pay attention to the ache, the impact, the anguish.

April tried to turn and run, but was halted, lifted into the air, wriggling, bashing her arms and legs back and forth.

The devil approached her.

Oscar pushed himself to his feet, sprinting forward, but the devil only needed to swipe his claw into the air for Oscar to fall back down.

The devil didn't even avert his gaze.

"I have been waiting," he directed at April, approaching her helpless, mortified body, "for a conduit like you. Someone with the strength to channel something stronger."

Oscar pushed himself to his feet once more, only to be brushed aside once more.

"And now I have you."

Oscar landed on his front, his forehead smacking the rough bumps of the gravelly surface. He wiped blood from his head onto his arm, ignoring the pain, forcing himself back to his feet.

They were inches from each other now, the devil and April – he was reaching out his claw, easily the size of her body, and stroking the underside of her chin like he was fussing a pet.

She tried to speak, but it was stifled.

She tried to scream, but her voice had been somehow lost.

She tried to breathe, but she suffocated.

All she could do was turn her head, ever so slightly, and lock eyes with Oscar. In her eyes he saw her apology, saw her fear, saw her despair – and he saw every reason he had to not give up.

"I will give you what I need to give you," the devil told her. "Then you are free to go. Free to return to your world."

"No!" Oscar screamed, dragging himself to his feet, his voice breaking under the strain. "Let her go!"

Oscar was pushed down again.

"Leave her alone!"

He tried to get up, but now he couldn't even do that. Something was pressing down on him, on the lower arch of his

263

back, flattening him out, pressing him to the ground, keeping him paralysed, unable to fight, to move.

"April…" he whimpered. "April… No…"

She continued to stare.

She tried to mouth something, but her mouth could barely move.

But Oscar could just about make it out; could just about see the syllables that completed the sentence *I'm sorry.*

The devil clenched his fists, straightened his back, turned his cocky grin to a triumphant growl that shook the ground, shook the lava, shook the sky. It all kept shaking, loose stone and gravel beginning to rise, and Oscar could feel it, something growing, some kind of power rising, something gathering, a crescendo of evil, coming together into a moment that was planned, waited upon, desired for eternity after eternity.

The devil's eyes narrowed.

His body stretched and altered until he was unrecognisable, until nothing remained but a large, thrashing mess of flames.

April straightened, rigid, every part of her like wood.

The flames soared toward her, aimed at her chest, sinking toward it, until the lashing of the fire spread, encapsulating her in its burning illumination that made Oscar have to turn away.

And, in seconds, it was over.

Oscar looked up.

The devil was gone.

April lay on the stone surface.

And he could move.

He leapt upwards, sprinted toward her, collapsing at her side.

Her eyes were open, but weren't moving. Blood dribbled down her nose.

"April," he said, shaking her.

Her head slowly turned toward him, so slowly he wasn't sure if it was real.

"April, please."

She shook. A little, at first, then her whole body rattled, trembling, until her seizure was such that he was unable to pin her body down.

Then her body fell, loose.

She began to rise.

It was like her head was being lifted by some invisible force, and her body dangled beneath her.

She floated upwards, floating away.

Oscar grabbed onto her leg, holding tightly, hanging beneath as they continued to float upwards.

She moved faster and faster, and he tried to secure his grip, using both hands, tightly around her ankle, so tightly, but he began to slip.

She soared faster, and faster still, until all of their surroundings became a blur.

Oscar clung on, gripping with all he had.

He tried climbing up her for better support, but it only made him slip, so he continued to clutch onto her ankle, retightening his grip over and over.

Everything went faster and faster and faster.

The fiery pits became an orange blur then left, as did the scorched sky, and they passed the white light, ascending at rapid speed, so quick Oscar had to turn his head away against the wind resistance.

But he did not let go.

He would not let go.

He closed his eyes and flinched his head away.

Then, suddenly, it all stopped.

He could no longer feel April in his grasp.

He opened his eyes.

Everything was a blur.

A frantically beeping machine was all he could hear.

Someone was shouting.

Their voice grew clearer, and he could finally make out a few words, *stay, calm, stop.*

His vision returned, and he saw someone he knew.

Lacy.

It was Lacy.

Stood over him, pushing him onto the bed, keeping him down.

He realised he was shouting something. He was shouting April's name.

"In a minute, Oscar," Lacy insisted. "You just need to stay calm, just need to stay still, just for a moment."

But he would not stay still.

Not until he saw April.

Not until he knew she was okay.

THEA WAS PROUD OF HENRY.

He had performed heroically.

But it was time to end this.

She felt something change. Something alter.

The balance had shifted.

Oscar's back...

Now it was time to find out whether she was the real deal or not – whether St Helen's and the orphanage had just been flukes.

St Helen's could have been a one-off.

The orphanage could have been luck.

But this would have to be her. Nothing else.

Just her, the strength of her gift, and a mass of bodies that remained stolen from their owners.

"Because from distress You have rescued me," she bellowed, "and my eyes look down on my enemies!"

Henry backed away. He'd done his part, he'd helped as much as he could, but she was glad that he was sensing it was the right time to give her space.

"Let these poor souls find You, a fortified tower."

They all huddled, all edged backwards, all backed away.

"Let the enemy have no power over them."

She raised her hands, held them high, looked over the possessed, circling so she could feed her words to all of them.

"I command you, unclean spirits, along with your minions attacking these servants of God!"

A few convulsed. Some fell. Some even tried to run.

"By the mysteries of the incarnation, passion, resurrection and ascension of His Son."

They were all on their knees now, all cowering, all trying to resist.

But resisting was futile.

"Obey me to the letter, for I am Hi s servant and you shall be emboldened to harm in any way a creature of God."

Every synapse, every cell, every twinge of muscle or rising feeling of sickness in her gut intensified, electrified – and came soaring out of her and over those who dared oppose.

"Those who come to judge the living and the dead by world of fire, release them."

She shook.

It was too much.

Her body was overloaded.

But she had to continue.

She had to know if she could do this.

"Begone, you hostile powers!"

Screams, moans, shrieks entwined with wails.

"Release them!"

It was too much.

She felt blood trickle from her nose and down her lips.

"Release them!"

Every muscle seized, every bone stiffened, and she rose ever so slightly from the ground.

"Release them!"

Then it left her.

She felt her head hit the grass, saw nothing but colours flickering as blurs.

She closed her eyes, then rested.

"Thea."

Someone was saying her name.

She closed her eyes.

"Thea!"

She opened them.

Who was that?

Who was with her?

"Thea, you did it!"

She forced her eyes open. Forced the blurs from her vision and forced her mind to reengage.

Henry was beside her.

She stayed on her back. Did not get up.

"It worked," he told her. "You did it. It was amazing, I don't know how, but – but you did it."

She peered from her space on the floor and saw puzzled people, some running away, some being sick, some just standing idly trying to remember what had happened.

"So I did," she said.

"It was so cool," Henry told her. "They all just, like, fell, and shook, and then you shook, and then they all shook, and their mouths opened and they all were freed, and–"

"Henry, Henry," Thea said, clearly not running on the same amount of adrenaline as him. "A little slower, yeah?"

Her head was thumping. Every movement of her muscles was a strenuous task. Each breath was a strain on her lungs.

But she had never felt stronger.

"Thanks, Henry," she said.

"What for?"

"I couldn't have done it without you."

He stayed by her side until all the people had left and it was safe to call an ambulance, ready to tell the doctors that she had simply fell and had a seizure.

After all, that's what had really happened – right?

5 8

Oscar pushed and batted Lacy's arms out of the way, but she was insistent.

"Oscar, stop!" she shouted.

"Get out of my way!" he snapped. "I have to see April."

"Thirty seconds, and you can see her – but you have been brain-dead for almost fifty minutes. If you get up without me checking you it could do some real damage."

"I. Don't. Care."

"Well, you asked me to do this, and I did – so sit down!"

He stopped struggling. She seemed to ignore his glare as she began feeling his forehead.

The machine was still beeping manically. It took him a while to realise that was his heartbeat.

He looked around the room, back and forth, searching for April, until he found her, lying on the sofa.

"Why did you let her do it?" Oscar demanded.

"Do you think I had a choice?"

"You could have stopped her. Told her it wasn't impossible. Refused to put her under."

"Oh, yeah, because that worked so well with you, didn't it?"

She put a thermometer in his mouth.

"What are you doing? This is wasting time."

"Shut up and stay still."

She stood over him, waiting for the machine's beep to slow down, which it didn't.

"Can I get up now?" he said.

"I wouldn't recommend it," Lacy said. "Your body has been through a lot of trauma and you shouldn't move for at least twenty-four hours. But if you are so damn insistent, then go ahead, what do I care?"

He pulled the pads from his chest. The machine indicated a sound like he was flatlining, but Lacy quickly turned it off. He ripped the IV drip from his arm and stood.

Immediately, he collapsed, his legs wobbling and giving way.

"Told you," Lacy said.

Ignoring her, he used the bed to drag himself to his feet, but the bed simply collapsed under his strength. He reached for Lacy's arm.

"I'm not helping you cause permanent brain damage, Oscar," she said, moving out of reach. "Get up yourself."

He reached for a side table and tried to use it to pull himself up, and he almost did, getting a glimpse of April's face, only to fall once more.

"Are you going to listen to me now?" Lacy asked. "Are you going to get some rest?"

"I will get some rest after I've seen April. Now please, just help me get to her."

Reluctantly, Lacy put his arm over her shoulder and helped him crawl to the side of the sofa, where she set him down on his knees.

Without a machine to tell her of April's pulse, Lacy put her two fingers over the inside of her wrist and waited.

Her eyes were closed. Her body still. Beautifully expressionless.

"How's her pulse?" Oscar asked.

"Really slow," she said.

Oscar felt her forehead and quickly pulled his hand away. It was like he'd put his hand on something just come out of the oven. He tried putting his hand back again, only to find it met the same resistance.

"She's too hot, I can't even touch–"

Lacy raised her hand to get him to shush, her eyes widening.

"What is it?" he asked.

"Her pulse is quickening."

Lacy's eyes widened and widened, and she looked more and more alarmed, until she was looking at Oscar, full of terror.

"What? How fast is it?"

"It – it's quicker than yours was when you woke up."

"What? How is that possible?"

"And it's getting faster, so fast I can barely–"

April's eyes shot open, and they both fell back as if thrown.

Oscar dragged himself upwards once again, pulled himself across the carpet toward her, and leant over her.

Her eyes were open, but she still didn't move.

He put his hand on her arm, and it was as stiff as a week-old corpse.

"What's going on?" he cried to Lacy.

Lacy came over and put her hand on April's wrist to feel for her pulse, but quickly withdrew, shaking her hand.

A burn appeared on the inside of her fingers.

"April?" Oscar said. "April!"

Her mouth curved upwards.

Her eyes slowly crept toward him.

Then her lips moved, and she spoke in a voice far deeper than April could ever manage.

"Hello, Oscar," it said.

THEN

59

"IT'S A PREPOSTEROUS IDEA, JULIAN!" DEREK INSISTED, STRIDING through the hallways of his home like he was searching for a room where he would find some sense.

"Why?"

Oh, Julian.

So young, so foolish.

Derek was grateful to have discovered him, and hoped it was just the beginning of his recruitment of Sensitives – but if they were all as reckless as him, he was in for a tough task!

"Because you can't just march down to Hell and kill the devil. It's a ridiculous notion."

"That's another thing I wanted to ask – like, he's called Satan, Lucifer and all that, yet you only refer to him as the devil. Why?"

"Because that is who he is, you silly boy."

Derek finally stopped in his study, where he leant on the desk and bowed his head. He closed his eyes and took a moment, an attempt to regain some semblance of patience.

"You are new, and you are inexperienced, and unknowledgeable, and I understand that – but you need to realise, the wisest is he who realises how little he knows."

"Derek, I'm just asking you the question."

Derek huffed, exasperated, scrunching loose sheets of paper left in organised piles on his desk.

"Fine," he said. He took the seat beside his desk and indicated with his hand for Julian to take the seat across from him.

"What is the question you would like to ask me?" Derek said, doing all he could to force sanity to his voice.

"It's just – we're fighting all these demons, yeah? And they all come from Hell."

"Yes, that would be correct."

"And you went to Hell in The Edward King War."

"We glimpsed it, entered it for minutes, albeit briefly, with Eddie able to get me out, and with devastating consequences – yes."

"Then why doesn't anyone just go to Hell and kill the devil?"

"And how would you propose one does that?"

"I dunno, like, take a knife down and stab him or something."

Derek sighed. Rubbed his sinus.

Where had he left his whiskey?

"For starters, you wouldn't be able to take an instrument into the other world. You'd be lucky if they granted you the dignity of clothing."

"So, strangle him, then?"

"We are talking about the devil! Do you not understand? The ruler of Hell, the one with dominion over the antichrist, the one who is made up of an evil so pure and so thorough and so calculated that it would be immeasurable and impossible to assume the perplexity of his villainy. No restrictions would be placed on the sins he could commit. And you want to strangle him?"

"Okay, so, one more question then?"

Derek told himself it was just an inquisitive mind, something he should encourage. After all, he'd had to learn all of this once.

"What is it?"

"Imagine, say, that the devil was unleashed. That he was set upon the world. Well, what then?"

"He would have to go through a mortal body and achieve amalgamation incarnation, and I'm not even sure a mortal body would be able to withstand him for that long, not unless it was a great conduit or–"

"Okay, okay, yeah, I get that – but what if? As in, what if he found a way?"

Derek sighed. Peered deeply into Julian's naïve, youthful eyes.

Ah, to be young and know so little. Some say knowledge opens doors; Derek says it's a burden. Sometimes he wondered if he'd be better off not knowing the things he knew.

"Then I couldn't possibly imagine the devastation that would occur," Derek said.

"Care to speculate?"

Derek sighed again. How could you possibly put such big, grand ideas into something as meaningless as words? There was no way to craft the semantics needed, no lexical choice or appropriate syntax he could find that could answer this question to its fullest extent.

So he tried.

"You want me to speculate what would happen, should the devil find his way into a human body, possess it, and achieve amalgamation incarnation – something considered to be nearly impossible."

"Yes."

"Fine." Derek's expression turned grim. "Tsunamis. Earthquakes. Genocide. The complete removal of the human race overnight, as a wave of disasters brings upon the apocalypse, leaving the world free for demons to be unleashed into it and no longer restricted to the depths of Hell."

"Oh..."

Julian sat back, deep in thought.

"That quite answer it for you?" Derek asked.

NOW

60

Oscar, Lacy, Thea, and Henry sat around the kitchen table.

Lacy sat back, biting her lip, staring catatonically at the untouched glass of water before her.

Thea chewed her bottom lip, glancing between Lacy and Henry, but not daring to look at Oscar.

Henry fiddled with his hands, staring down at them and not once lifting his gaze.

Oscar, however, didn't notice how everyone else was positioned. He was sat with his elbows on the table, his chin resting on his clasped fingers, staring at nothing in particular, lost in deep thought.

He knew he was going to have to go up there eventually.

He knew he was going to have to face whatever it was.

He knew he was going to have to identify it.

He just… he had to wait, first. What for, he wasn't sure. Guts. Gumption, maybe. But if it was confidence he awaited, he was going to have to wait a very long time.

"Lacy," Oscar stated matter-of-factly. "I want to thank you."

He sat back. Took a big, deep breath. Looked to his left where Lacy sat.

"I know you did not want to do this," Oscar continued. "I know how much of a struggle it was. I know how much Jenny meant to you and me using her to persuade you probably wasn't fair."

Lacy flinched at Jenny's name. Oscar was astonished that, all these years later, she was still wounded by losing the one she loved.

"I think this could be an opportunity for you to gain some closure, maybe. To find a way to live a life that isn't shut away. You've still got time. Either way, I am grateful for your part. You did everything I asked, and no failure of the task was put on you. You were great. Sincerely, I mean it – thank you."

Lacy gave a gentle nod.

Oscar turned to Henry, sat to his right.

"Henry," he said. "What you did a few days ago was stupid and foolish. It showed me that there was little point training recruits. It showed me that many couldn't be trusted, and we would not be able to use them to win this war."

Thea went to speak in his defence, but Oscar raised his hand to stop her.

"But what you did last night proved me wrong," he continued. "I know how tough it was for you to enter into battle. I know how hard it would be for you to overcome all of your reservations, to find a way to fight, despite already losing so badly. Thea has told me you were magnificent, and you helped keep the battle outside, and away from where we were. So, Henry, I thank you."

Henry shifted slightly. Apart from this, he did not react.

Finally, Oscar turned to Thea.

"Thea," he said.

"Oscar, honestly, you don't have to–"

Oscar raised his hand to silence her and continued anyway.

"I was starting to wonder if the concept of a Sensitive with a stronger gift was obsolete. Having found no obvious function within this war, I wondered whether it was a success that would lead to nothing more than that – a minor success. But, I am glad to say, I was wrong again."

He leant forward.

"You did so much last night. And not just from your gift – you were the leader when others couldn't find the strength to be. You were decisive, making the right calls at the right time. You were everything I needed you to be yet had never asked you to be. Thank you, Thea, so much."

"Oscar…" Thea said, as if she was going to say more, but she ended up leaving it there.

Oscar looked between all of them.

"Now," he said, "you are all dismissed. Your service has ended, and you are free to live your lives."

"What?" Thea snapped. "Oscar, we can't just–"

"The last plan we had failed. The world can't be saved. It's done."

"There has to be a way."

"There was. For me to defeat the devil. In that, I failed. I am sorry, but that is how it is."

"Oscar, we aren't about to abandon the fight. Until the end, remember?"

"That's the thing, Thea. It already is the end."

Oscar stood. Pushed his chair under. Meandered to the doorway, where he paused and turned back.

"And what about April?" Thea asked.

"I will find out what demon was put in her. I will battle it, defeat it, and free April. Then we can sit, hand in hand, and watch the world end together."

"Look, if all we have to do is defeat the devil, then–"

"*All* we have to do? Don't you get it? There is no defeating the devil. He can't be defeated. It is *impossible*."

Thea huffed. Looked around. Tears were in her eyes.

Oscar was so fed up of tears.

All he ever saw in people's eyes anymore were tears.

Damn those tears.

"And what about helping you defeat whatever's in April?" Thea said. "Surely you'll need help."

"I'm the best exorcist still alive. I'll be fine."

He turned to go.

"Do you want to end up like me?" Lacy said. "Because you're going the right way."

He paused at the bottom step.

Turned.

Looked at a woman who could have done so much more than she had, if only the circumstances had favoured her.

"I'm far beyond where you were," he told her, and left, taking the steps slowly, one by one.

He really didn't want to climb them, go upstairs, or enter that room.

But he had no choice.

He could hear the screams as he grew closer. April's screams, her voice shrieking, in there somewhere, surrounded by a great many other voices, a multitude of wails.

Yet he knew there were only two inside that body – April, and whatever the devil had put inside of her.

He paused outside the door.

Checked his pockets for his rosary and his crucifix.

He didn't need the Rites of Exorcism anymore. He knew them.

He knew them all too well.

He placed his hand on the door handle and paused again.

Here we go.

He opened it and entered the room, a room so cold he could see his breath on the air.

He flinched at the wretched sight. April, tied to the bed, her face so different from her own it was unnerving. The sweet smile and soft cheeks and clean, silky hair were gone – replaced with a cocky grimace, a pale canvas of wounds, and matted grease sticking in clumps to her head.

She looked so unlike April, so drastically disgusting compared to what he had come to love. It made him gag.

But he couldn't show weakness to this demon.

Couldn't show it anything but his best.

He walked to its side, took the rosary from his pocket, kissed it, and placed it around his neck.

He took the crucifix, and just held it.

Its eyes followed him everywhere. Fully dilated. Bloodshot. A tinge of red.

"Oscar," said April's voice. "Oscar, please help me."

Its mouth didn't move at all. It sneered at him, her voice tiny and hidden inside, as if it was letting her cry out, letting her speak without moving its cracked lips, as a taunt, as a way of teasing him in the most hurtful way.

He had to stay calm. Collected. Cool.

He couldn't let it win. Couldn't let it get to him.

"Oscar, what are you doing…"

Still its lips didn't move, still her voice came out between them.

"Oscar, it's hurting me, it's hurting me."

"Shut up," Oscar snapped.

He couldn't help it. He reprimanded himself straight away for the stupidity.

"What's the matter?" came April's voice, the lips still not moving. "Can't take a little joke?"

Oscar wiped his brow. He was perspiring quite profusely, despite the freezing temperatures of the room were making him shiver.

"I am speaking to the entity that dwells within," Oscar said, holding out his crucifix.

"He doesn't want to speak—"

"Shut up! Stop using her voice, I know it isn't her!"

Again, he mentally scolded himself for the impudence, the downright recklessness of letting it get to him.

That was how it would win.

And he couldn't let it.

Hundreds of exorcisms gone, yet this one was more than tough. It was torture – and he had come to know the meaning of the word *torture*.

"Who am I speaking to?"

"April, my name is April. Would you like me to sing you a—"

"Enough. Tell me, what pathetic demon am I talking to?"

Its grin spread until April's mouth had widened unnaturally, dispersed across her cheeks until its edges almost met her eyes.

"I am no demon," it said, this time in its own voice.

"You don't fool me," disputed Oscar.

It laughed a low-pitched, growling laugh.

"All this experience and you still know nothing," it mocked.

"I know enough to know that you are a demon."

"I am not just a measly demon."

"Then what are you?"

It cackled.

"What are you?"

It cackled harder.

"I said *what are you?*"

"You still haven't figured it out…"

"Tell me what you are, so I can send you back to where you came from."

"There is no sending me back, Oscar. You've been to where I came from. You think I put something else in her?"

Slowly, it began to dawn on him.

Slowly, it all made sense.

Slowly, he saw that a situation that could not be any worse had steadily become much, much worse.

"No…" he gasped.

"Yes, that's it… figure it out…"

"You lie!"

Yes, that's right.

Demons lie.

It's what they do.

It was claiming to be him, pretending, doing it to hurt him, to mock him, to taunt him.

Though he knew that wasn't true.

This was just denial rearing its ugly head.

"Do you know who I am now?" it said.

"No," Oscar replied, wanting to hear it for himself. "Tell me."

Its grin widened even further.

"My boy, I am the devil," it said.

RICK WOOD

UNTIL THE END

THE
SENSITIVES
BOOK
EIGHT

WOULD YOU LIKE TWO BOOKS FOR
FREE?

Sign up for Rick's Reader's Group at www.rickwoodwriter.
com/sign-up and get two of his books for free!

ALSO AVAILABLE BY RICK WOOD

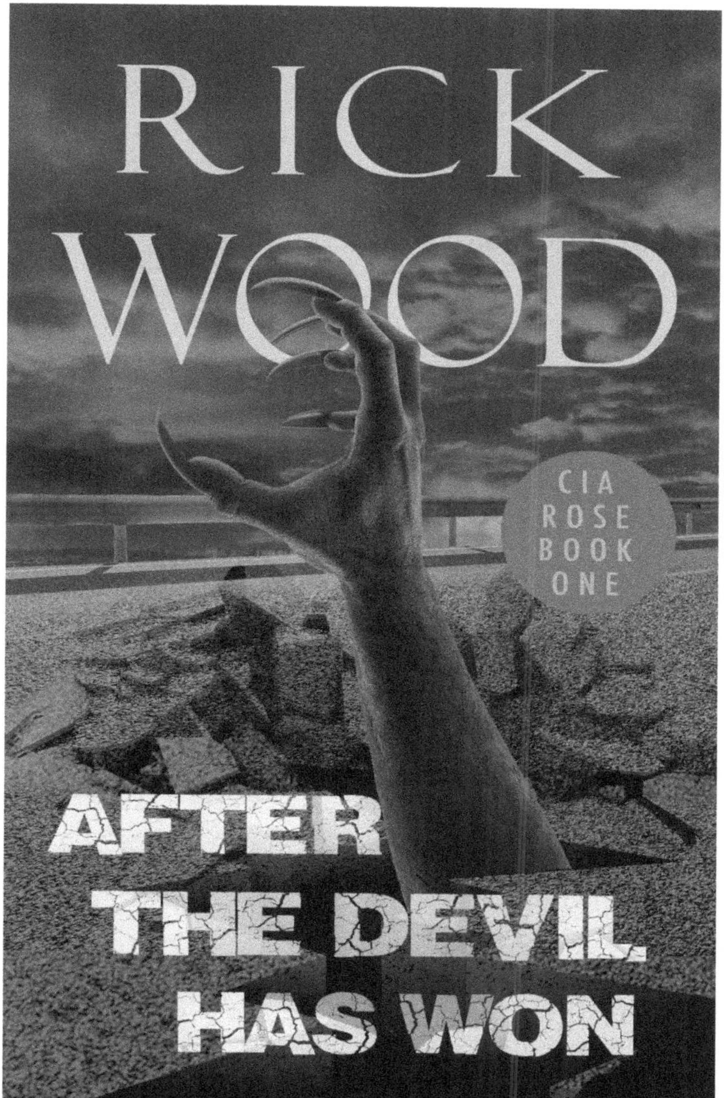
RICK
WOOD
CIA
ROSE
BOOK
ONE
AFTER
THE DEVIL
HAS WON

RICK WOOD

SHUTTER HOUSE

BLOOD SPLATTER BOOKS

18+

PSYCHO B*TCHES

RICK WOOD

CPSIA information can be obtained
at www.ICGtesting.com
Printed in the USA
BVHW032136120321
602480BV00006B/74